The Wilderness

D.N. STUEFLOTEN

FC2
Normal/Tallahassee

Published by FC2 with support provided by Florida State
University, the Unit for Contemporary Literature of the
Department of English at Illinois State University, the
Program for Writers of the Department of English at the
University of Illinois at Chicago, and the Illinois Arts
Council. Sponsored in part by the State of Florida, Florida
Department of State, Division of Cultural Affairs, the Florida Arts
Council, and the National Endowment for the Arts.

Address all inquiries to: Fiction Collective Two, Florida State
University, c/o English Department, Tallahassee, FL 32306-1580

ISBN: Paper, 1-57366-087-6

Library of Congress Cataloging-in-Publication Data

Stuefloten, D. N. (Donald N.), 1939-
    The wilderness / D.N. Stuefloten.--1st ed.
        p. cm.
    ISBN 1-57366-087-6
    1. India--Description and travel--Fiction. 2. Cochin (India)--
Description and travel--Fiction. I. Title.

PS3569.T843 W55 2000
813'.54--dc21

                                                    00-021097

Cover Design: Polly Kanevsky
Book Design: Michael Benton and Tara Reeser

Produced and printed in the United States of America
Printed on recycled paper with soy ink

Contents

PREFACE

I began *The Wilderness* in 1964 in Africa, in what was then called Southern Rhodesia. I was 25 years old and working for a magician. I had already been wandering for some years. I had worked my way through the south seas on a fishing boat, and taken a motorcycle up the center of Australia. Moro pirates smuggled me into Borneo, where I ran a small mining company. In those days life seemed an accumulation of adventures. I carried with me a typewriter, an old Underwood, balancing it on one shoulder. I remember using it as a weapon in Bombay, beating away an angry taxi driver. A red-haired girl watched me. Do you carry that with you everywhere you go? she asked, nodding at the machine. Everywhere, I said. Then you are always armed! she cried. In Africa I drifted south, alone and hungry. At the Zambezi River, at the border between Northern and Southern Rhodesia, the magician hired me. It was there that I found the first sentence, the first image of what became my first novel.

The book was finished something over a year later in southern California. How does one reconcile the long dusty roads of Africa with the concrete highways of America? Perhaps one cannot. The American army drafted me, court-martialed me, and ejected me. Draft notices had actually been trailing me for some time, across Australia, Borneo, India, and at last were reinforced by the threat of revoking my passport. What would my life have been like without a passport? Once free of the army, I finished *The Wilderness* as quickly as I could, put it in a box, and headed south. It was a relief to resume wandering. I traveled by canoe up the Usumacinta River, taught English in a girls' college in Costa Rica, hitch-hiked to Panama. Soon enough I began other novels. *The Wilderness*, however, pleases me in ways the others do not. I see dancing among its pages the nimble fingers of my youth. It has lain quiescent for thirty-six years. I am glad to finally have it published.

D. N. STUEFLOTEN

PART ONE

I.

I am confused by the purple mountains in my memory. I am confused by the woman who lies on my bed, dead after so many years of suffering, her skin turned purplish by the twilight. I am confused, also, by the total lack of people around me, and this is strange: have I not, all my life, sought to partition myself off from everyone else? Have I now, indeed, through some power I never expected, banished the world from my presence? It is all the more bewildering, since, casting back in my mind, a tremendous multitude of people pass before me, all colors and sizes, people who crawled over every corner of the globe. For it is true, I am sure of it, that I have been everywhere. I cannot imagine one river that I have not seen, or one mountain, or a single desert that I have not crossed. The names of these places are like islands in my memory. Katmandu, the Australian Bight, Nurye Elia, Sibutu, and thousands of others, towns and villages, hills and mountains. Either I have been to these places or I have imagined them so violently that they seem true and real to me, as real, or even more, than the room where I now seem to live, with its bed and chair and barren floor. I cannot explain this to myself, not yet; I do not know if I have placed myself here, or if someone, with power greater than mine, has placed me here, imprisoned me perhaps. I have made experiments, to be sure: the door, for example, is locked: but have I locked it to keep others out, or was it locked to keep me in? It is impossible to say. The woman, when she appears, asprawl on my bed, will not answer questions. Or perhaps the questions I ask her have no answers, and silence is her only possible reaction.

There are others, too, which I must mention at the outset, since they may have an important bearing on my plight. I have not seen them for a long time, it seems like years, but I am not deceived by the apparent extension of time here, where every minute seems an hour, every hour a day—it cannot have been more than two weeks. But I will only mention them, and leave further descriptions for the time when they again appear. It is more important, I believe, now that my memory is functioning, to write of those visions that appear from my past. There were times, for example, when I took direct and irrevocable action which resulted in some change in course, for myself and others. Of these incidents several stand out, one of which occurred in that dry and discolored area in the south of India. The town was Cochin, on the coast, full of those little winding streets typical of all Indian towns, with dirt and dust everywhere, and little men wearing skirts. Because, perhaps, it was on the coast, it did not smell as badly as the inland towns, which are full of urine and shit from both men and animals. I do not remember how I had gotten there, but I was proceeding towards the post office, for in those days I occasionally received mail, and as I walked through the crowd an Indian on a three-wheeled trishaw rang his bell alongside me and gestured at the seat in the carriage behind him. I shook my head, since I had little money and could not afford the luxury of riding. But he, small stringy dark fellow that he was, persisted. Where is Sahib going? One rupee, one rupee only. As a joke (I had not talked to anyone for days) I said, Ten naye pais. No, no, he said, still ringing his bell, and immediately dropped his price to eight annas. I talked to hear myself. Your bell is out of order, I said, the seats are filthy, you are not strong enough to take me to the post office.

All right, he said. Get in.

Ten naye pais? I said.

Yes, yes! Get in, Sahib!

You are a fool and a liar, I said, your children are cursed, you would eat cow if you had a chance, you are the dirty illiterate son of thieving parents.

Get in, Sahib!

Ten naye pais?

Yes, yes, I take you there!

You are as worthless as a cunt on a goat, I said, but I will get in.

The carriage rocked, and the little man strained away, tucking his skirt in at his waist, ringing his bell at all the people crowding the roadway. When we reached the post office, I got out and held ten naye pais in my hand for him. He stared at it.

What is this, Sahib?

This is your ten naye pais, you black idiot.

No, no, Sahib! One rupee! One rupee is the price!

It was only what I expected, so I turned my back to him and entered the post office. There were rows of barred windows and brown people milling about. The coolness made me feel light, my head floated, and the only thing that kept my feet on the floor was the tugging of the trishaw driver at my elbow. His fingers were hard and persistent; they were shaped like claws, and like a bird he fluttered about, clicking his teeth at me. I had rupees in my pocket, seven of them, and with everyone staring at me I could feel my hand descending into my pocket, as a matter of habit; it would require almost no effort to separate one rupee from the others and hand it to him. In the coolness, the lightness of the room, it seemed the normal and logical thing to do; I was being persuaded, by the clutching hand, by the sea of brown faces around me; but as I was on the verge of actually doing this, the sun suddenly came through a window, and everything rose up in my throat. The dust from the floor, composed of dirt and manure, filled the air. Men were spitting, and a naked child was rubbing his penis with a tiny fist. A sari-wrapped woman, darkened in a corner, picked her nose with a jeweled finger. I turned to look at the trishaw driver, and for the first time saw that his eyes were rimmed by parasitic worms, and his lips were open over black teeth and a black tongue. Each long, stringy arm was waving in the air, and his toes were scrabbling in the dirt. A vision of futility and suffering took hold of me, my life and his, his hungry belly and my hungry soul, each eaten by acids and ulcerated by frustration. My mind vanished. I saw him not as a man, but as a blackened rose, and towards his charred throat my hands moved. I saw them in front of me, at a curious distance, with veins that seemed to be branches on a desert tree. There were sandy dunes around me, a wasted land. There was a blister of heat in the sky. The trishaw driver, now a rose, tumbled end over end through the air until the ground leaped up to meet him. For a moment nothing moved. Then a crowd of people drifted into view. They huddled dark in the corners, their mouths open, their hair black and oily. The rose became a man. Dust lifted into the sky. Shadows darted into hollow cheeks. A long murmur spread around me. The wind blew me outside, and, useless scrap that I was, the wind blew me down the endless street.

The barrenness of the country has infected my brains. The tale, in the telling, has disappeared from my mind. But if my memory is gone, other things have become clear. While I was writing, a man came in, bringing me food, and immediately I realized that I have seen him many times before. Miraculously he did not look at my bed, where the dead woman lay, but only placed the food on the table, where I was busy writing, and without looking at me further, left the room. I distinctly heard a key being turned, and when I checked the door it was again locked. While I ate, other things came back to me. If the distant past has vanished from my memory, the affairs of the last few days and nights have returned. I know, for example, that there is a key in my pants pocket which will unlock the door. Outside, in the other rooms, there live three people, two men and one woman, who have their meals on a bare wooden table little better than mine, except for the older man who last night I saw sitting in a corner, eating a plate of curry with his hands. He was an old man with a red face and white hair, and he was the only one who saw me. But his eyes were milky and empty, and it is debatable whether he actually saw me, or if his vision just passed over me. The old woman and the young thin man did not look up from their food. The old man grunted as I passed beyond his sight, and I heard the woman smack his hand with her spoon and begin a bitter tirade against his helplessness, to which the old man merely responded in a sort of chuckle: Heh-heh-heh! When all was quiet again I opened the door leading outside and leaned against the wall, breathing in the cool night air. On the wall, at that point, I found marks, designs carved into the stone, and grease from hair, that convinced me that I had spent many evenings just like this, leaning on that wall, watching the evening traffic of bullock cart and dogs and stray men. Passing me, calling up at the lighted windows, were peddlers and hawkers, trying to make their last sale before retiring. The men called out and joked with each other as they slowly walked down the street.

Hey there, one would cry, are you still selling last week's fish?

There are three pretty girls down the street who would like to buy something from a husky man like you!

Hey, old man, you had better sell some of that load before it crushes you!

Watching them, something began to stir in me, and with some astonishment I tried to examine it. I took my body apart, piece by piece. There was a movement in my bowels, something warm and light in my stomach. Deep in my chest a rose-colored heart flapped away, and I could feel a liquid rushing within my arms. For a moment it frightened me, it was so strong, this quickness and lightness I felt. But then I recognized it, and with a bound the word leaped forward: joy. I did not know what to do. Valuable minutes I wasted, unable to react, and then, as my lips shaped the word, the crowd thinned out, the jostling and joking disappeared, the night yawned down cooler, and a slight wind began to pick up the dust and blow it into the air; and I was unable to hold the word. It slipped from my lips. I grabbed at it, but too late; the night descended around me; down the street a thin man in a trishaw came furiously pedaling; he careened from one side of the road to the other, the frame of his bike bouncing and rattling; and behind him, drawn into the vacuum he left, I saw the prostitutes of the city peering from their doorways, their silken robes shining. Thin, milky arms picked up rocks and tossed them, with a strange gentleness, at the trishaw driver, who ducked and swore and turned livid with his effort. As he came closer, I saw the reason for his hurry. In the seat behind him sat a huge, bald man, holding a whip which he cracked over the driver's back. The bald head gleamed in the moonlight, and the face was set and implacable, never changing expression. When the trishaw driver passed me, he stared at me grimacing with agony, and I saw that his eyes were rimmed by parasitic worms, and his mouth black and empty. Then, in a rush, he was past me. And after him the prostitutes stepped out into the road, drifting by in their cool silken robes, smiling at me.

II.

My memory leaps from moment to moment. Sitting here in this room, I try to use this pen and these scraps of paper as a leash, but it is useless. I am lost, I know that, and all these words will never bring anything back to me, but if by putting these images into some form I can grasp an understanding of what has happened—I do not know. There are so many things, all jumbled together, things I cannot be certain of, conversations I may or may not have had, it seems hopeless. The woman rises and falls, her breath grows hoarse and rapid, I see, in the darkness, her body twisting on the ground. And yet there is nothing around me, an empty room. The young man who lives here looks at me oddly. The old woman seems frightened and angry, and the old man, her husband, grins and points a bony finger at me. Heh-heh-heh! he says. I know you! The old woman does not talk to me, and yet, when I first came here, she fawned over me, I can remember that, her thin, light body bowed almost to the floor, and she snapped commands at her son who laconically brought me a glass of water, a bowl of curry. During the weeks, or months, whichever it has been, she has drawn back, and her son, so distant at first, has become almost friendly. Yesterday again he asked me my name. I could only smile. Call me what you like, I said.

But where are you from? he persisted. Are you English, American, perhaps Australian?

I waved my hand airily.

I have been to all those places, I said.

Surely you have a passport. All foreigners have passports.

What are you trying to find out? I asked. What do you want to know? Why do you ask so many questions?

I am only trying to help you, he said.

Your mother does not like me.

She is proud to have you here.

And your father?

He knows nothing.

And so I know no more than before. I have been here so long, I will never leave, I no longer have the strength. When I first came, I took long walks, but my legs have grown curiously numb. I have not ventured out since that time, two weeks ago, when I followed the trishaw driver through the city. I was standing outside when he came by, pedaling slowly, his chin sunk onto his chest. I edged back into the shadows, so he could not possibly have seen me, and yet, as he came abreast, his head lifted and turned in my direction, and he gave me such a sad and knowing look, and at the same time such a scornful one, that I felt myself shrink and burn, as though I were a dried leaf in the August sun. He did not look behind, and yet I followed, and knew that he was aware of it. He went slowly, through the late afternoon, and I treaded silently over the shadows. There were few people about, it was too hot, they would appear with the cool of the evening, and I saw only a beggar or two, an old woman wrapped in a shawl, a child sprawled in an alley. A few dogs watched me pass, their tongues drooling. I smiled as pleasantly as I could. My red skin shone in the sunlight, my hair was white, my beard a dirty yellow. The streams which flowed through the city, and which that afternoon we passed, smelled of urine and shit and dead, decayed bodies, for the people died everywhere, their bodies lay for days in the streets, in the water, wherever they breathed their last. I slowed, and stopped, and stared, but always the trishaw driver kept his slow pace, and at times I had to hurry to keep up with him. He led me through the winding streets until we came to the outskirts of the city, and chose a path that led into the low hills surrounding. When I saw where he was going, I stopped. The hills were yellow and brown, they were virtually deserted, and the path I saw was rutted and overgrown with weeds. In the heat it was difficult to think. My face was burnt and sore.

Where are you going, old man? I asked.

And you, I said to myself. What are you up to?

Behind me the city glowed and trembled. My feet started up again, and with a sigh I followed.

As we went through the hills, the shadows lengthened, and here and there I saw the remains of old houses, shallow excavations in the ground, stone-lined basements and the ragged edges of walls. Sometimes I saw dogs slinking about, mangy curs, their fur ripped from fights and disease. Shortly before the sun went down, the trishaw driver left the path and bumped over the open ground. Ahead of him was a tree, and next to the tree a small shack, nothing more than a lean-to, built of old branches and palm fronds. In front of the doorway sat an Indian woman: I could see her dark, squatting form as she worked over an open fire. Behind were children, three of them. The trishaw driver stopped pedaling, and got off his machine. The woman stood and bowed to him. He disappeared into the shack, and I stopped, uncertain of what to do.

After a moment he reappeared and looked in my direction. He was holding something in his hand, and stood there, waiting. As I approached, the woman got up and bowed again. She had tattoo marks on her cheeks. The trishaw driver held a bowl out to me, and I took it. It held that thick, brutal liquid called arak that the people brewed for themselves. As I drank it my head became dizzy, and I was grateful when the man sat down, so I could sit also. Together we sat there and waited, while the woman prepared the meal.

We sat there, the three of us, a stringy, diseased man, a tattooed woman, and myself.

After a while he brought out a clay pipe, and I smelled the sweet sharp odor of hashish. He handed the pipe to me, and I had a few puffs, and gave it back.

And yet, the night was curiously empty. The woman glowed red from the fire, her dark limbs cluttered with markings. Behind us I could hear the three children scurrying about; somewhere in the distance a dog barked; the trishaw driver sucked loudly at his pipe; but I was off, alone in the blackness, my mind wandering about over the earth like a wind, picking up dust and bits of paper. I relaxed, and drifted. I swayed, like those trees in Borneo when the monsoons came, and the warm and rushing rain fell everywhere. I drifted over the Masai plains, along dirt roads, listening to the chants of the savages, the orange-draped women stamping their feet. It is easy on nights like that to disappear. I disappeared, and wandered, and it was pleasant, because no faces intruded, her body did not appear. A fisherman threw a net in the sea. I plunged into the water, and swam down along the vertical face of a reef. The trishaw driver sucked, his pipe glowed red, the woman shuffled her pots over the fire. A dog crawled into the light, his moist nose sniffing. Pot-bellied children lingered in the background. I crawled through a gutter in Intramuros, while a fat whore tickled my belly, and tiny dwarfed people stared at me from their holes in the walls, their scraps of houses. A policeman shouted with laughter, waving his pistol in the air, and in Pasay he (or another one like him) shot a man who folded across the belly and sat down, making whumping noises deep in his chest. The wind picked me up, and moved me along. A train rattled and rumbled through a tunnel, and I sang, loudly and off key, while an Indian boy clicked pieces of wood like a castanet. It all went through and around me. I could smell the sweet hashish, the trishaw driver smiled, she did not appear, not once, I recognized that in the back of my mind, she was missing even from the Masai plains and Arusha and the nameless little village where she died. Instead of her there was the tattooed woman, handing me rice and a bowl of grease with shreds of meat floating in it. I drank more arak, and the trishaw driver puffed away. The children squatted on the ground, sucking at their food. The woman stood behind the trishaw driver, picking lice from his hair and throwing them into the fire, where they popped and sputtered. The gold ring in her nose twitched when she smiled. The lice sailed through the air, and sizzled in the flames. The man and I got up, he carrying his pipe, me with a bowl of arak, and we went off into the night and urinated on the same bush, his penis long and black, mine thick and red.

Together we walked, he slow and uncertain from his drug, I clumsy from my drink. The fire dwindled away into a tiny pin-prick hole in the darkness, and the stars, one by one, popped into view over our heads. Together we crashed through the brush, holding each other up. His skirt became tangled in the thorns, and laughing I jerked him free. Then we found ourselves in a little valley, shaped like a cross in the hills. Down it a tiny stream trickled, made of silver. The trishaw driver went onto his knees, and for a moment I thought he had collapsed, and I reached down to help him. But then I saw he was praying, praying and puffing on his glowing pipe, and I stepped back, fearful of intruding. His thin body fell flat onto the ground, his fists clenched, and he beat himself about the shoulders and head, never saying a word. I drew my meagre clothing about me. The man rolled over the ground, and then stopped, still reclining, and fastened his shining black eyes onto me. One hand extended and pointed: next to him was a small grave with a little chip of wood stuck into it. It was too dark to read the inscription, but I knew the name on it. All my laughter vanished. The hills were huge. I was small.

It's not true, I said.

The trishaw driver rolled again and came into a crouching position, his eyes never leaving me.

Youre lying, I said. It's impossible.

His mouth opened into a grin.

You bastard! I said, kicking stones at him. It was thousands of miles away! She cant be here!

Heee-heee-heee! he screeched.

You fucking bastard! I shouted. I'll kill you!

Heee-heee-heee! he screeched again, doubling and twisting with mirth. I jumped on him, but like a snake he squirmed from my grasp, and I went rolling over the black hills. I stumbled to my feet, and saw him leaping and prancing. I fell down, and his laughter cut me. He laughed for a long time, while I crawled after him, but then he disappeared. There was no sound anywhere. Even the hills were speechless. I stayed there the rest of the night, on the warm ground. It was impossible to move. Instead I dreamed about her, about the opening of her legs, her slow shuddering passion. I dreamed she was sleeping beside me, her eyes and fists tightly clenched. During the night she moaned in her sleep, and then her tiny voice cried, Where are you taking me! What are you doing! And her little fists, in her sleep, struck me, again and again, helplessly, while I lay there, unable to move.

III.

And yet, I betray myself. My mind betrays me. The thousands of miles I have traveled are useless.

I do not know the name of this city. I arrived on the back of a lorry, and when I saw its dark and crowded streets, its beggars and its prostitutes, the blinding heat, I thought: This is where I can stop. I could lose myself in the noise, in the cheap taverns. I admit it, I was tired, I had traveled far, without sleep, without enough food, and I was looking for an excuse to stop; but nevertheless the city was attractive to me, sprawled out and disorganized as it was, its streets without names. I squatted at the side of the road, smiling at the people. Beggar children gathered around me, and they demonstrated their infirmities. A boy held an arm with a huge, running sore in my face, and I nodded at him, and with great solemnity gave him two copper pennies. A legless child I gave four coppers, and the idiot with the crossed eyes, three. It was not long before there was a huge crowd of them pressing in on me. Children, I said, children, the world has corrupted your bodies. They shouted for my attention, but I held up my hand. Children, I said, I am a modern man, a product of western science and cleanliness, a carefully nurtured biological specimen of another world. Sahib! they cried. Sahib! No, no, I said, children, my coppers will not cure you, and I am out of miracles, I have lost them already, all my education, my studies in western schools and universities will not help you. Sahib! they cried, jumping up and down. Sahib! Bahkeesh, Sahib!

A trishaw driver stopped in the street, ringing his bell at me. When I got in, he smiled at me in recognition.

Ah, it's you! I said.

Yes, Sahib. Where does Sahib wish to go?

To the cages, I said. There must be cages here somewhere.

He grinned widely.

Yes, Sahib!

And get that grin off your face!

He tucked his skirt in at his waist, I waved goodbye to the children, who were still plucking at me and imploring, and we started off down the street, the trishaw gathering momentum. The bag which contained my spare clothing was tied with a rope, and I pretended it was a whip, and cracked it over the driver's head. He peered over his shoulder at me, grinning toothlessly. Hyah! I shouted. Hyah! We whirled around a corner so fast I thought we would turn over, and I grabbed the side of the swaying carriage. Hyah! I shouted. Then he screeched to a halt at the edge of the road, ringing his bell, making the people jump out of his way. We are here already? I asked. Yes, Sahib! Look! You see the places? And it was true, so I got out. The trishaw driver clasped his hands together, grinning at me, his face shining with sweat. You are a good man, I said, you are very strong for such an old, stringy fellow, look, I give you two rupees instead of a few annas. The man bobbed and nodded his head. Thank you, Sahib!

There were children here too, and like a visiting prince I scattered largess among them, foreign coins, bits of copper, sens and cents and centavos. I dodged them, but they came shouting after me, and I was forced up the steps of the nearest whorehouse, up above the cages, where I saw peering from a ground level window a broken face with long black hair. I walked slowly up the narrow stairs. It became cooler, and darker. The wood was unpainted and splintery, and looked as though it had been formed of old orange crates and discarded scraps of lumber. In the large room at the head of the stairs were mirrors and three vases with red flowers. There was a small rug on the floor, and on the rug a low table. Around the table, on sofas and a few chairs, sat the women, twelve of them.

The first was wearing a faded housecoat, tightly buttoned. Her feet were broad and flat from going barefoot, each toe like a round little head, spread away from its neighbor. Her legs were dirty and scaly.

The next two were peasant girls from the country, with mustaches and hairy bodies. They were holding hands and suppressing giggles.

The fourth had a harelip and a sullen smouldering face.

The fifth looked part Chinese and had granulated cheeks. She wore tight pants and blouse, and she was short and stubby.

The sixth was a simple girl with a clumsy body. She smiled with her head down.

The seventh was a small girl in a dress much too large for her. She had bright eyes, and was looking at me directly and eagerly.

The eighth wore tight pants also, but she had long legs, she affected shoes with high wooden heels and used makeup on her face. Her lips were very red. Her eyes were darkened and scornful.

The ninth wore a silk sarong, and her features were pleasant and smooth. Her feet also were flat and dark. Her body was heavy.

The next two were uglier than sin.

The twelfth was the mama of them all.

I was the only customer.

What, I said, is this? A wake? Let us have some music!

The mama gestured, and one of the ugly girls turned a dial on a radio and simpered in my direction. The music was Indian and loud.

My god! I said. To stand that I need some fortification! A bottle of beer, please!

The mama rose to her feet and clapped her fat hands and called out in her own language. A sleepy boy appeared in a doorway. She spoke again, and then sat down and ignored me until the boy reappeared, bearing a bottle without a label. He opened it, and I sniffed at it. It was green and frothy. And how much, I asked the mama, do you want for this concoction? She sniffed. Three rupees, she said. Ah, I said, never let me be the one to argue with a lady. I gave her the three rupees, which she stuffed between her breasts, and the boy poured the beer into a glass and shuffled from the room. I drank it slowly, and it had no effect on the music, which bounced off the mirrors and howled through the doorway and down the corridors. The little flowers in the vases were drying out. Their edges were brown and the petals drooping. The hot sun outside would turn them to dust in seconds. Inside they lived on borrowed time, sucking at their meagre supply of water, blinking at the electric, cold light. The women ignored me, except for the two ugly ones, who continued to simper in my direction, and the girl in the silk sarong who glanced at me, looked away, and glanced again, and the girl in the overlarge dress, her small body restless, who stared at me with bright eyes. The mama appeared asleep, her hands folded across her belly. The one wearing lipstick and high-heeled shoes had brought out a cigarette, and puffed unconcernedly, her tightly encased legs crossed. The harelip looked as though she were getting ready to spit at me. The simple girl with the clumsy body stared about vacantly. The two peasant girls next to me were still holding hands and looking into each other's eyes, giggling. The one in the housecoat drummed her feet on the floor. The one in the oversize dress leaned forward, and her breasts nearly spilled from her tight, dirty-white brassiere. Come, I said to her. We go talk in your room, ai? I picked up my beer bottle and the glass, and went over to her. She was sitting next to a vase of flowers, and when she rose I plucked a flower from the vase. It was tired and drooping in my hand, but the girl had sparkling eyes and a restless body. We went down a corridor to a little room, large enough only for its bed and a small table and a pan of water on the floor.

I put the flower between her breasts, and she giggled.

Here, you sit down, huh? she said.

And she took my glass and filled it and brought it to her lips.

Is all right?

Is all right, I said.

She drank a little, refilled the glass, and handed it back.

You want talk to me, no? See if you like?

She pulled her dress to her hips and climbed onto the bed, putting one knee on each side of me and squatting across my thighs. Peeking at me from between half closed lids, she pulled her skirt higher, and pulled down her panties. See? she said. She let go and the panties snapped back against her belly. Hmm, I said. My goodness. Youve got something there, havent you? She pulled her shoulders together, and her dress slipped down to her waist. The flower tickled my nose. The edges of her brassiere were dark with sweat, and through the thin cloth I could see the dark sweaty shapes of her nipples, two of them, swinging on the ends of her breasts. How about that, I said. You like, no? she asked. I like, yes, I said, and she rose slightly on her knees and swiveled her hips, with steadily increasing pressure, across my groin. Her dark hair swayed alongside her cheeks. Her eyes were shining and laughing, and her lips puckered, her teeth, what teeth she had, as brown as her skin.

And so I was caught, as I had planned, past the point of return. The days on the road had dried and withered me, the lorry had been full of dust and sacks of manure, the hours waiting in the sun had boiled my brains and choked the tubes and vessels and intestines and passages of my body. I paid her the money, twenty-two rupees, and then like a magical well she opened up, full of strange liquids, smelling strongly (under her armpits, between her legs) of curry and spices; a quick little animal, crawling over me and breathing in my face, shedding her garments (and pulling mine off) as she came. The room was dusky, the dying sunshine drifting in through a single dirt-coated window, making gray shadows on the wall. And what was it like? What did I feel? A plump little body, the warm throat of a vagina, tighter than the one in Colombo, wetter than the one in Mombasa; a little different from the Malay girl in Kuala Lumpur, who had worn a red silk sarong, thick and cool under my fingers; less noisy than in Tai-o-hai, less impersonal than Manzanillo, not as dangerous as in Sibutu, where she breathed quickly and with fear behind a palm tree, in some bushes; plumper than the girl in Kota Belud, not as pretty as the whore in Zamboanga; one bigger, one smaller, each different and each alike; and all of them related by their sex to the girl who died, clutching herself with sharp fingers, in a village on the Masai plains. The dust from the plains filled the air, the wind had been blowing hard for three days: but the dust dropped and vanished, here in this room, brought down by the last thrust of a penis and a white gluey bundle of semen.

IV.

Outside, the trishaw driver was waiting for me, but I ignored him and walked on down the street. As I turned from him, I caught a glimpse of his face staring at me in astonishment.

Sahib? he said plaintively. Sahib?

He tinkled his bell and pedaled slowly after me.

Sahib? he repeated. Sahib?

But I was not interested in him, the cages held my attention, the road full of dark people. The two story buildings looked ready to fall over or collapse upon themselves. Between the buildings ran alleyways and rising from them were crooked clattering stairways. They were familiar to me, the cages, I had seen them in Bombay (where she had accompanied me, her face turning ugly with astonishment and disgust and fear) and Calcutta and alone in Kuala Lumpur, where I had spent a rough and drunken night walking through the mud, trading insults and comments with the inhabitants (Apa mau? I asked the old one who stuck a long bare leg in front of me. Saya mau orang puh-tee! she chanted), awakening in the morning behind one of the little shacks, so stiff I could hardly move. It was then I decided to go to Australia, a white country, where I was to meet her. I drifted through the jungle to Singapore, expecting to find something opening up for me; but it took eight months to reach Sydney, through Borneo and the Philippines, crawling in a kumpit through the Sulu Sea, eating dried fish and drinking straight rum. Little green islands rose out of the ocean. The water was full of purplish jellyfish and sea slugs. In Sibutu a Moro family of smugglers took me in, and a young Catholic priest gave me wine and listened in astonishment as I told him of my travels. He must have slept badly that night, dreaming of silken Malay girls and the ragged hungry urchin-whores of Alexandria. The next day he would not speak to me, and I went on to Tawi-tawi, and from there to Zamboanga and Cebu City, where there were cages, of a sort, also, with plenty of whores in tight dresses and fine, light, San Miguel beer. The cages here were Indian in character. Above the cages were the whorehouses. In the cages were strange dark creatures, staring from their barred windows, some toothless, some scarred, their hair like string; they fixed their black eyes on me, and their mouths opened into grins. Behind them I could see bunks, not beds, blankets over boards, and in each corner a pan of filthy water. Through one window (her customer must have just left), I saw one of them squatting over her pan, her dress tucked in at the waist, splashing the water at her crotch. Her eyes were burning, and her legs had melted into strange shapes, the right one only a bone with no flesh attached. She limped to her window and leered at me. And past her and all the others milled the people, blind to their charms. Darkness drifted into the street, carried around the corners and into the cracks by the wind. A few trishaws clattered down the way, and a taxi came bumping up, disgorging a few young Europeans. (Ah-ha, I said to myself, I must be near the ocean, these men are sailors, I can tell.) Their white skin and tall husky bodies made strange shadows on the street. They were met immediately by two pimps, who took their arms and guided them down the street. And it was not long before I too was approached. He came alongside me, a half step to my rear.

Sahib? he said. You wish to find nice young girls?

No, I said, I have already found nice young girls. Now I wish to find a place to sleep.

But Sahib, he said, there are no hotels here.

If I wanted a hotel, I would not be here.

He blinked his eyes in surprise.

Sahib, I do not understand.

I have merely stated, I said, that I do not wish a hotel, and that I am looking here for a place to sleep.

Does Sahib wish to stay all night with girl?

No, Sahib does not.

Then I do not understand. Does Sahib wish a taxi?

No, Sahib does not wish a taxi.

He walked beside me a moment, frowning.

Sahib, I know plenty nice girls, very nice place close by.

So does Sahib. I am merely, solely, and simply looking for a place to sleep.

But Sahib, is too dirty here!

27

Dirty? I asked. I have been all over the world, my friend, and I have slept in many dirtier places than this.

He was silent for a moment, and we kept walking.

What does Sahib wish me to do?

Sahib wishes you to dig a hole and bury yourself.

He laughed uneasily.

Sahib, you are joking, of course.

I never joke.

But Sahib, you cannot walk here all night, and you cannot sleep in the streets.

Perhaps not.

Sahib, I know many families here, they are very poor and very hungry all the time. Their houses are not like your houses, and they have very little room.

I need very little.

Sahib, for a white man, it is not good.

And yet it is what I wish.

Sahib, please understand, I know very little of this. Sometimes my friends have people stay, but they are dark like myself, and sleep on the floor, and it is only a few annas. But you are white man, and you must have bed, and room all to yourself.

It is preferable. Twenty rupees for one week.

A week, Sahib!

At least.

Sahib, it has never been done!

That means nothing. I will wait here, while you inquire, no?

But Sahib, you must not!

Go! I will wait.

Glancing uneasily over his shoulder, he left.

And so that was how I came here, to this room. It was not difficult at all, but then nothing has ever been difficult, except living. Details of the practical sort never clamored for my attention. It was something she could never understand. When I traveled from one place to another, how I could get there never interested me, and what I would do unimportant. But with her, traveling meant arrangements made in advance, bookings and telegrams. Without these she faltered, her nerves became voracious and hungry. I worried instead about the sun and the earth and the shapes of the stars, the smell of the wind, the faces glimpsed in passing. What could be more important than the exact hue of the sky or the touch of the sea on a hot body? That evening, walking through the streets with the pimp, the sounds of the city were burnt into my mind. Children were crying out, an old man was singing, and wailing over his voice was the loud music from a wireless. My shoes made clicking noises, but the young man at my side glided softly, his bare feet big and bony. At the house three people met me at the door, but the old woman shoved the man back out of sight. She smiled and nodded her head. Her feet scraped nervously at the floor. Her son watched me quietly and suspiciously, his eyes dark and luminous, the eyes of a deer. The woman was the master of the house. The white-haired man grinned toothlessly in the background. She showed me to my room; I had the impression it had been quickly vacated; the bed, which she patted proudly (why did she talk so much, in two languages at once?) bore the image of someone's body, not in the coverings, which had been smoothed over, but in the duskiness of the air hovering above it. There was a table on which I already had the urge to write, and a stool which had once been a chair. She called, much too loudly and with too many words and gestures, at her son, who had remained leaning on the wall opposite the doorway. Slowly, very slowly, his shoulder left the wall, and when he walked away his body leaned forward before his feet moved, each half of him moving separately. He returned, hours later, bearing a glass of water with a scum of grease on its surface. I drank it and lit a cigarette, onto which her eyes lighted like a hawk. When she and her son (she dragged him along) led me to the urinal, in the alley behind the house, her eyes never left the glowing tip of the fag. At the urinal, which was a tar pot

fenced off with scraps of wood, she was flustered and hurried; the place was evil with urine and shit; a dog scratched
on the fence, whimpering. Back in the room her son slowly
brought me a bowl of curry, and left. The smell of the curry
destroyed what fresh air had been in the room.

Enough, I said. I must sleep.

As I gave her the money her husband appeared in
the doorway, peering at me. She withdrew backwards, bow-
ing, and when the thin door shut I heard her slap him, and
her voice quivered and sliced at him. A dry rasping sound
was barely audible over her noise. Heh-heh-heh! he was
saying. Heh-heh-heh-heh!

PART TWO

I.

My room is a dungeon; I have banished myself. But the decision was taken so long ago, it is difficult to remember the reasons. Outside, through my single window, I see only haze, and at times, late in the afternoon, the red dust that comes sweeping through the sky. There are never any birds, they do not come here; the land is dead. Only the persistent flies, the insects, flock around this city, in numbers that seem to grow each day. I stare through the yellow glass, and wander about the room with my eyes. On the walls I find a map of the world: the continents, the oceans, the inland seas, black rivers, icy mountains, the sandy hills around Aliminos Bay, the jungle around Lahad Datu, the flat, diseased land at Exmouth Gulf, the peaks of Nuku Hiva; they are written in the urine stains, the broken plaster, the long cracks that wind through valleys and gorges, along the discolored countries. What is there to say? I have been everywhere. I find the red-painted Masai plains; as I look out the window, the dust covers the sky; people are chanting in the streets. Outside, the wind blows, there is the trembling song of hungry people, the buildings crack and sputter and twist back and forth to escape the rushing air. Once, walking through a stormy day (the wind hot, never cold, the clouds yellow with dust and not black with rain), I found a bus nosing its way around the corners. It came sniffing up to the trucks and trishaws, it beat its way through the crowds of people, brushing at the wooden shacks, purring and snarling and coughing. Its motor cowlings were black with oil. Its windscreen was littered with dead bugs. The driver I could barely see, his eyes squinting, his head darting back and forth. At his throat he wore a yellow scarf, but I could see the knob of his Adam's apple bobbing up and down. In the darkened interior of the bus were rows of people. As the bus passed me, hardly giving me a glance, I saw the pale faces pressed against the windows. There were old men and old women. Scattered among them were young faces, bland and empty. One face was half hidden by a black camera; and the set of the chin, the color of the hair, the shape of the lips—I hung motionless above the ground and said to myself: So she is not dead after all. The heat was painful. The sounds of the city disappeared; gone were the wailing music, the clattering of feet, the babble of hundreds of voices. Then she lowered the camera, her eyes passed over me, and the bus roared as the driver changed gears. A baby began to cry. My arms ached. I allowed the sweat to trickle down my face.

Even if it were, I said.

A beggar woman smiled at me.

Further ahead the bus had stopped.

I stretched my arms and looked around; the beggar woman remained at my side, poking me with her extended finger. Well? I said to her. What should I do? It is a matter of keeping calm, of staying rational. She nodded her head. Down the street, gathering around the bus, came children and old people dressed in rags. I could hear their cries and the faint rumble of the bus engine. Obviously, I said, they are stopping for photographs. It was an old Western custom. The girl was a tourist; she was passing through. Do you agree? I asked the old woman. And again she nodded her head; her dark eyes looked slyly at me. On her cheeks and forehead were painted little red teardrops, and on the backs of her hands were dark tattooed lines. She was a little, gnarled, tattooed woman wrapped in a shawl and sari, a dirty brown rag, with a toothless mouth and dark sly eyes. I dug into my pocket. A rupee, after all, meant little or nothing to me, a meal or two perhaps. It was more valuable in her hands than mine. When I gave her the money and walked on, towards the bus, she followed quietly behind me. At the edge of the crowd I stopped. Ahead of me was a young boy in tee shirt and short pants; ahead of him a crippled man; and then a dark head, a waving arm, a pair of bright eyes, and the bus: old, covered in dust and grease, the sides painted blue and white, squatting on the road with its huge black tires, the motor cowlings clattering with the vibration of the motor. And the wind passed over it all. It kicked up the dust and made flags of the old saris and shawls and flapping shirts. It came heavy with the odors of the street, curry and sweat and excrement, and blew in gusts against the foreign bus. As I watched (listening to the cries, picking out words here and there—Bahkeesh! bahkeesh!), the windows of the bus snapped down, almost in unison, and a whole series of faces peered out. And over the crying people I heard a loud voice:

Throw them a penny, dear.

Behind a gray haired woman, an arm made a tentative gesture.

No dear, said the voice again, dont be foolish, that's a shilling. Throw out a penny now, that's a dear.

Her lips turned into a brittle smile, and all along the bus black cameras clicked. I edged back, into a windy shadow.

Throw out another one, dear, I want another picture.

Filthy buggers, said a man.

Pennies and threepences came from the windows. How can they live in such a state? said a woman. Animals, said a man, bloody animals. I watched the people: their arms reaching, ducking, dodging, the heads bobbing down and up, their bodies pressing together. Standing apart from them, leaning against a building, I saw an old woman. Between her legs crouched a small child, his eyes bright and staring. The woman raised an arm covered in silver bracelets, and gave a shrill cry, and immediately the child darted into the crowd. Just like monkeys in a zoo, said a man with a red face. A white-haired woman smiled prettily. I'm getting such interesting pictures, she said, wont you throw out another penny? I found the girl again. The wind was making her hair fly in front of her eyes, and a small hand kept brushing it away. Her camera rested on the window ledge. Her gaze moved over the people, her eyes wide; at another time, in another place, I had seen such a gaze before, mixed with bewilderment and sadness: staring at a crowd of people in Intramuros (people living in caves in the thick walls; sharp ribs, thin faces; the cluttered shacks with people squatting in front of them), a girl had said, Why must they live like this? She had no camera. Uncertainly she moved down the street. People began following us. Why must they live like this? she said again, and I took her arm. She recoiled from the beggars. Later the gaze turned to disgust: in Madras, perhaps, or even Djakarta. But the girl in the bus looked back and forth, the wind tossing her hair, until her eyes met mine, and then she quickly turned away. And the white-haired woman—the same one, perhaps, whose husband (or father, lover, friend, dear enemy) had thrown out the first penny—said in the same loud voice: It's all very fine, of course, and I'm sure very educational, but one neednt linger so, dont you think, dear? And obediently the bus coughed and rasped into motion again, and the windows all snapped shut. The crowd began to melt, they ran off in all directions; and standing a few paces from me I found the old beggar woman again; she was looking at me with her black mouth opened into a smile. She said something in a quick low voice to another woman, and then both looked at me and grinned. I inclined my head. Excuse me, ladies, I said. I walked on up the street.

It was late afternoon, but the air had already cooled down, and in spite of the wind the streets were full of people and traffic. I saw beggars, old women, children sprawled in alleys. Dogs watched the bus pass, and then turned towards me. I smiled at all of them. I nodded my head. My skin took on the redness of the sky, and my beard turned a dirty yellow. The big bus, clumsy and uncertain, rumbled right and left, it crossed a narrow bridge and approached the old park. The stream under the bridge smelled of urine and shit and dead, decayed bodies. The park was dry and yellow; in the evening the queers gathered there, I had seen them, dark liquid bodies moving in the night. Families lived there also; they lay like littering sacks in the dust, under the trees. Large dogs loped through the bushes, nosing at the people. Then the bus slowed; across from the park was a whitewashed hotel, and the bus pulled to a stop in front of it, the motor dying with a black cough of smoke.

I squatted on my heels and considered the bus, the people who descended from it, and the hotel courtyard they entered.

A dry palm tree scratched at the wall of the building.

A man tried to sell me colored postcards. I shook my head.

Very good, Sahib, he said. You buy very cheap.

It's tea time, I said.

Yes Sahib, very good, I make good bargain.

What would I do with them? I asked.

Oh, many things, Sahib. You send to your family, to all your friends. They like very much.

What's that hotel like? I asked.

That hotel, Sahib? Very nice place. You want, I take you there and show you.

No thanks, I said. I got to my feet. The man nodded in front of me, the colored pictures held in his hands. I can still walk, I told him. They serve tea there?

Yes, Sahib, they serve tea, whatever you want. But I can show you better place with plenty of girls.

No thanks, I said again.

I shook him off and crossed the park. The trees and the dust did not stop me. I walked past the bus, counting my steps, and paused at the iron open gates of the courtyard. But a wind pushed me through, and carefully averting my eyes, I walked forward until I found an empty table supported by curled iron legs and surrounded by four empty iron chairs. Everyone, no doubt, was looking at me (a wind and sun burnt apparition), but I looked at the red sky and then lowered my gaze to the top story of the hotel: yellow plaster. Small, square windows with bars in front of them. Yellow-green palm trees rose almost to the roof, and under them, in the shade, were the other tables. Mine was the only one in the sun. The heat floated down and rested on the top of my head like a warm bird. Then a dark man dressed in white came from the dark interior of the hotel. He walked up to my table and stood there. He was an old man, his face was leather, the sun and the wind had eroded it. During the dry season he had to brave the dust. During the monsoons, the rain would beat at him. Tea, I told him. Yes, Sahib, he said. For one? That is agreeable, I replied. If Sahib would prefer the shade, he suggested. I shook my head. I preferred the sun. He turned and walked away, threading his way past the tables and the people. The wind kicked at his heels. The voices of the people littered the air: sweet, gentle sounds compared to the roar outside. I turned to look at them.

At the nearest table sat a bald man and a gray woman.

At the next table sat a man with red suspenders, into which his thumbs were hooked. With him were two women, both wearing cloth sandals and dresses with flowers printed on them.

Near them, opposite the courtyard from me, sat the bus driver with the girl I had followed. He had his yellow scarf. She had a blue dress and fine brown legs and tanned arms. He was leaning forward. She was leaning back and smiling distantly.

Further away, at a table by themselves, sheltered by a single tree, sat two old women with plump bodies. They wore identical straw hats shaped like volcanos and tied under their chins with string. Both had fans which they wielded listlessly, stirring the air: the wind, beyond the walls, was dying, and the gusts which reached within the courtyard were erratic and devilish, like the breath of a hot beast.

I leaned back and began to dream. What else was there to do? I sat alone among strangers. But the dream (a bright sky, a grassy hill) was interrupted by the appearance of a dog. He was small and yellow. His legs were covered with ticks, and fleas were jumping in his fur. He came through the gateway and nuzzled at my legs. He walked very stiffly, as though his tick-covered legs would not bend. His ass went up and down as he walked, and he occasionally took several steps sideways, as though drunk and unable to keep his balance. His eyes were encrusted with yellow muck, and very sad. He looked up at me, yellow-eyed and sad, but I had nothing to give him. His moist nose sniffed at me. Then he went to the bald-headed man and tapped him on the foot. The man looked down, angry, his face red, but the woman smiled and made pretty sounds. The bald-headed man gave the dog a biscuit and kicked him on his way. The dog ate the biscuit listlessly. A swirl of dust approached him, and he stared at it, his tongue hanging out. When the dust hit him, he shut his eyes and quivered. A couple of fleas were carried away, but the ticks held grimly on. Then the dog trotted stifflegged, forwards and sideways, to the man in the red suspenders. The man opened his mouth loudly. Hey, boy! he said. What's up, eh? Looking for a bit of a handout, I bet. Ho-ho! Wouldnt make much of sheep dog, would you, eh? One of my wild Aussie rams would probably kick the daylights out of you, eh boy? Here, take this, now git, go on now, atta boy! The dog moved on. It's marvelous how these people weave, isnt it? said the woman at the man's right. I've had arthritis since I was forty, said the other woman. The dog munched on the biscuit, and then threw it up. He coughed, his thin belly heaving, and stood there for a moment, spreadlegged. Then he trotted over to the driver and the girl. The driver snarled, but the girl reached down and patted the dog. Poor little fellow, she said. Then she saw the fleas, and jerked her hand back and made a face, and the driver kicked the dog away with a curse. The girl started to say something, but then frowned and turned away. Her eyes met mine. The dog moved again. He went over to the two old ladies. They sat there, their eyes straight ahead, fanning the listless air. Their hair poked out from under their straw hats. The dog tapped their feet with one paw, but they just fanned away. Above them the sky was yellow and red with dust. The dog settled at their feet, let his tongue fall from his mouth, shut his eyes, and did not move. The two women fanned the air.

You are unhappy, I said across the distance. The girl continued to look at me. Her eyes were tired. It would be easy to walk up to her and take her away from the bus driver. You dont belong here, I could tell her. But she didnt belong outside either; nor did she belong with me.

The waiter brought me tea and little biscuits. His fingers were long and wrinkled. His white uniform was spotted with food. On the table he placed the pan of biscuits, a pot of tea, a pot of hot water, a pot of milk, and a bowl of sugar.

Are all these people staying here? I asked him.

Only a few days, Sahib, he said.

What is it? A tour of some kind?

Yes, Sahib. They are on their way to England.

Ah, I said to myself, an overland tour, no less. How daring. The deserts they had yet to cross would broil them. They were already, I thought, becoming familiar with dust and heat and flies. The bald-headed man looked cranky, and the driver nervous and irritable. I smiled at the girl, and she half smiled in return. Softly, softly, I said. I withdrew. I poured my tea and busied myself with the sugar and biscuits. I could hear the roar and mutter of the world outside the walls. The sky hung above everything, restless and hungry. Then two boys came through the gateway; they came from the world without, to the world within. One was hardly more than a baby, he could hardly walk, he had a dirty face and bright eyes. Both children wore only brief shorts, and were barefoot. The older boy's feet were broad and flat. He was shaped like a board, straight and thin, his skin very dark, but the belly of the youngest protruded suddenly in front of him. He tottered, the older boy walked. He walked straight up to the two old women who were fanning the air. They ignored him. He stuck an arm in front of their faces, but they closed their eyes and briskly moved their fans back and forth. After a moment he gave up, looked around, and then went to the table with the bus driver and the girl.

When he put the arm under the bus driver's nose, the man leaped to his feet with a curse.

The girl's face twisted with pain.

I got up and walked to their table. Ignoring the man and the girl, I took the boy's hand. Let me see it, I said. The boy grinned at me, his teeth white, and tossed his long hair out of his eyes with a quick movement of his head. The bus driver stepped back half a pace. The girl was watching me. Her dress was blue and clean, as blue as the sky in another country, and her features were smooth and fresh. The boy's arm was puckered with eruptions. From each sore ran rivulets of juice, caked with yellow dust. The arm was colored black, red, and yellow. What is it? said the girl. I shrugged. Malnutrition, perhaps, I said. That's what it usually is. None of them get enough food. I gave him a rupee. The grin widened, and he darted away, going to another table. The bus driver cleared his throat, and his Adam's apple jogged up and down. He was a thin man, his shoulders stooped. Shouldnt be allowed, he said and cleared his throat again. Not in a place like this. They serve Europeans here, y'know. We pay extra for it, and then they allow riff-raff from the streets—it isnt proper. I continued to ignore him and turned to the girl. Well? I said. Her eyes looked startled. Shall I join you? I said. She blinked her eyes. Oh, I'm sorry, she said. Yes—please do. And a smile made her face lovely and sweet.

I sat down.

The kid has worms, I said. The youngest one. When you see a dog or a kid with a belly like that, theyve got worms.

He was sitting in the dust in the middle of the courtyard, his pants pulled down, his little hands throwing dirt at his big belly.

What can you do? said the girl.

Nothing, I said. Half the children here have worms. The other half have something else. Ulcers on their skin. I dont know what they call it. Crippled. Rickets. It's a lovely place for diseases.

How awful, she said.

I daresay, said the bus driver, his throat working furiously. I daresay. But one hardly expects, in a place like this—he stopped, his face turning red, his eyes fixed on me—riff-raff! he exploded at last. Riff-raff!

The boy was standing at the table with the two women and the man in red suspenders. Hey-hey, the man was saying, go on, git, none of that now! The arm came closer with its sores, and the man hastily reached in his pocket for a coin. The woman next to him said, You can get some marvelous bargains in these bazaars, dont you think? The arthritis is especially bad at night, said the other woman. The boy triumphantly pocketed the money. The little child sitting in the center of the courtyard peed in the dirt. The hairless man rose to his feet. His face had been getting darker and darker; the sun beat against him, and his feet thumped at the ground. Big splotches of sweat appeared under his arms, and the woman sitting with him started squirming in her chair. Her hands were fidgeting with the cups on the table. When the boy neared him, the bald man lifted his fist and shouted. The sun glanced off his face. He was shining red. The boy stuck his arm under the man's face and cried: Yaah! Yaah! Then he grabbed some biscuits from the table and darted away. As he passed the two old women, he saw the dog, and gave it a kick. The dog lifted into the air, tumbled over the grass, and staggered to his feet. He stood there while the boy ran out, and then vomited some more cookies. His belly heaved up and down, and then he toppled over onto his side. The waiter ran from the hotel into the courtyard, his arms in the air, shouting in his own language. The little boy was still sitting and playing with himself. The waiter kicked him, and the child flipped over. He got to his feet and stared. He tried to walk, but fell down. At last he crawled out the gate, his pants still down around his knees.

The bald man slammed his fist on the table. All the cups and saucers rattled.

II.

I watched the silence gather round. It came nuzzling up to me, brought by a gust of wind, rubbing against my cheek. The people sat unmoving and quiet; perhaps in their somnambulant state they did not breathe; they were only bundles of clothes, feet, hands and heads, sitting at their tables in the courtyard. Outside I heard a man mournfully calling, and the bell of a trishaw as it tinkled down the street.

Nice friends you have, I said to the girl. The palm trees rustled in the wind. The day was dying, slowly, its blood flowing around the horizon. Do you live here? the girl asked. I nodded. Do you have a job? the bus driver asked, leaning forward. No, I said. No job. Not I. I had worked before, though, and often, at all sorts of jobs. I was a grape picker, a miner, a truck driver. I fought fires in California and fished for tuna in the Tuamotus. I was driving a semi during the wheat harvest in South Australia when I met the girl: she taught school in the town. After school let out she would come to visit me, and correct papers in my little house until I came in from the fields or the granary. On Saturdays she went out with me while I sewed sacks of barley or made a trip in the truck. Is it hard to travel, the way you do? she asked. No, I told her. It only needs patience. You have to get used to the crowds, the smells; sometimes you have to sleep on the ground, on wooden benches, in Sikh temples, whatever's available. The food was often bad, but I didnt want her to get fat. I slapped her on the rump. She rolled over in the grass, and we wrestled for a while, until it started getting serious. Not here, she said. Look how dirty you are! Tease, I said. That's all you do. I'll catch you later, and see what happens then. Wait till you have a shower, she said. Then see who catches who. When we went in, the boss asked me how many bags I'd sewn that day. Two-fifty? he said. Is that all? Yesterday you did three hundred. I laughed. There were distractions, I told him. He turned away, grumbling a little. But I was a good worker, so he didnt dare say too much; there was too much work, too little time; the fields all ripened at once. When the season was over, I said to her, Why not? Let's go. We've got some money. She turned away. I dont know, she said. It's such a big step. I havent put in my resignation yet. But I talked her into it; I wrote the resignation, she signed and mailed it. We went to Fiji, Suva, and rode up and down the green hills on bicycles. Then we went to Manila. In a hotel there we drank tea. The day was hot. We havent much money left, she said uneasily. What can we do?

What do you do when you run out of money? the girl asked me. Or are you rich?

She smiled at me. She was curious about my beard, my clothes, her eyes were trying to figure me out. The bus driver scowled, sitting stiffly. People were getting up and going into the hotel.

I work, I said to the girl. When I run out of money, I work.

You make it sound so simple, she said. What sort of work do you do?

You name it, I said. I've done it.

I imagine, said the bus driver dryly.

In Manila we drank tea in the hotel. I can get a job in Borneo, I told the girl. I know some people there. So we caught an inter-island boat to Zamboanga and Jolo and finally to Sibutu, where I knew a Moro smuggler named Haji Aba. He was a big man, wore a turban wrapped around his head, and spoke broken English and Malay. The Sulu Sea was gray in the morning and green in the afternoon. As we traveled across the ocean, we saw green jutting islands and purplish jellyfish in the water. We were dirty and tired. We ate dried fish and drank brown water. By the time we arrived in Tawau, she was sick, but after a while she got over it—there was a hospital in Tawau, and even a Danish doctor—and taught English in a Chinese school. I worked for the PWD as a road inspector. We watched the monsoon rains come sweeping in over the hills.

And is this what you do? the girl asked. You just travel around, and work here and there?

That's about it, I said.

How marvelous! she said. I cant imagine anything more exciting!

The bus driver turned away.

It's getting late, he said.

Oh, it's not so late, she said. Besides, I want to go to that fete tonight.

She gave me a speculative look.

In Tawau we had government quarters. It's lovely here, she said. I'm so glad we came. It was worth it—even that horrible ride from Manila. I dont ever want to leave. But when the Colony became independent, she became worried. The Indonesians were causing trouble at the border, and British troops were flown in. I worked up and down the roads; I inspected the graders and the bulldozers and the Bailey bridges. We ought to be moving, I told her. You ought to see Jesselton and Kuching and Singapore. Youll like Kuala Lumpur. Penang was a lovely island. The sea was calm, the world huge; a person shouldnt stay too long in one place; there was too much to see. Dont you ever want to settle down? she said. I shrugged. I looked at her long hair. She sat with her legs curled beneath her, like a little girl. She pouted at me. All you ever think about is moving, she said. Someday, I said. Someday we'll quit. But not now. On weekends we went out to an isolated beach and swam in the nude. She loved the ocean and the sun. It's glorious! she said. I'll never wear a bathing suit again. Never. But soon she would ask me again, Why dont we settle down somewhere? And I would tell her: I've traveled since I was a kid. I dont want to stop now. I'm not satisfied. Not yet. So finally we took a boat to Kudat, traveling deck passage. She didnt mind, the boat was large and uncrowded, and the situation at the border worried her; and from Kudat we went overland to Kota Belud and Jesselton, and then caught the ship again to Kuching and Singapore.

Arent you ever going to stop traveling? the girl asked.

Maybe I'll stop here, I said.

She wrinkled her nose in distaste.

What a terrible place to pick!

The driver looked around nervously.

Really, he said, we should go in for dinner. Sorry, he said to me, but we really cant invite you in. I'm afraid—they do have certain standards of dress, you know.

Oh, nonsense, the girl said. Why dont we just go to the fete and eat something there? I'm sure theyll have some kind of food. Would you like to come?

Why not? I said.

Dont be foolish, said the driver. You cant just eat out in the street. You dont know what youll get. It isnt safe in these countries.

Isnt it? she asked me.

I shrugged.

That's where I eat, and it's never made me sick.

It's settled then, she said getting to her feet. She looked at the driver. Are you coming?

You cant do it! he said angrily. You dont know these countries. Youll come back with—God knows what!

She made a face at him.

Dont be such an old sack, she said. Are you coming or not?

He stared at me for a moment, his Adam's apple working in his throat.

No, he said. I'm not. I'm going inside. And if you know what's good for you, youll come in too. You cant trust the people you meet out here. Thieves—the streets are full of them. Youll be sorry. Remember that!

Yes, father, I said.

His face grew dark; then he turned and strode away.

I'm sorry, she said, putting a hand on my arm. I cant imagine what's wrong with him.

Cant you? I said.

We went out to the street. She smiled at the passing people, the old lumbering buses. The trishaw driver pulled up, ringing his bell. Shall we? I said. Oh, she said, I've never ridden in one before! The old man smiled at us, nodding his head. Straight ahead, I think, she said. It's only a couple of blocks. Her legs were brown and slender, but strong too, and she wore sandals with high heels on them. You must swim a lot, I said. The driver strained away at his pedals, and we moved down the street. How did you guess? she asked. I pointed. A suntan, I said, and good muscles. She wrinkled her nose. Theyre fat, she said. She jabbed at her calves. A girl isnt supposed to be strong. The driver's back went up and down; dogs slunk away from under the wheels and a naked child stared at us. Music came from wirelesses, and here and there cookfires were burning, the blue smoke slowly rising into the darkening air. The girl's shoulder brushed mine, and she smiled at me, her teeth small and even. When she talked I could see her red tongue. Her eyes had picked up a sparkle, and she held her head to one side, like a coquette. I'm really glad I came on this trip, she said. But sometimes it's so depressing, dont you think? I'll be glad when we get to Greece. I've always wanted to go there. Further down the street I could see banners covered in script and a crowd of people. I think that's it, she said, pointing. Look at all the people! She drew back a little. Do you think we can get through them? she asked. Easy, I said. A string of firecrackers went off, and the people swayed backwards and forwards. The trishaw driver looked inquiringly at me. I nodded, and when we stopped, helped the girl out. Thank you, Sahib, the old man said. He grinned at the girl. Take it easy, I said to him. He nodded and backed the trishaw away.

The girl peered forward at the people.

I dont know if we can get through, she said.

Would you rather go somewhere else?

No, she said hesitantly. I'd like to see the priest again—he's the one who told us about the fete. If we can find him.

I took her hand. Let's go look, I said.

There were pinwheels and firecrackers. The people were dark and lean, their black hair falling before their eyes. We pushed our way into them; some of the men stared at us, others smiled, and some ignored us; elbows jabbed into our sides. I held the girl's hand tightly. I could smell grease and curry and sweat, and everywhere there was noise, music that wailed and wavered, the clatter of games and tin cans being banged, and voices raised in shrill protest or laughter. We fought our way past a booth, and watched a boy throw a baseball through a hoop. He danced up and down, and when he got his prize—a picture of a saint—he vanished. The crowd swallowed him. A fat woman in a sari shoved her way past me. A man shouted in my ear. A nun, holding colored darts in her hand, smiled from behind a booth. She had a lumpy brown face, but further on there was a white nun, in the same black costume, and her face was lumpy too. Everywhere we saw pictures of the saints and drawings of Mary and the infant Christ. The faces were smiling and stern, dark and light, with gold halos over their heads. I stared at them, and they stared back, expression-less. Elsewhere there were crucifixes and rosaries. The beads shone in the electric light. The girl was pushed against me, and when she looked up into my face, she tried to smile. I pulled her after me. Coarse cloth rubbed against my arm. A greasy head rammed me. On either side, high in the air, I could see the buildings, dark and silent. Like canyons they said nothing, but the sounds of the fete bounced off the walls and swept back over us. Then we were free. We found ourselves on the far side of the fete, among stragglers, figures in twos and threes, who were hurrying into the crowd. The sidewalk shops were motionless around us. The girl brushed at her hair and smoothed her dress. She looked around in amazement. Such a crowd! she said. The moon had appeared over the city, and from its light and the light of the electric lamps, her face went through changes in form: dismay and alarm, and then laughter and smiles; her eyes dark and luminous, and then sparkling, and then sad again. Where do they all come from? she asked. People leaped from alleys and windows. Dogs ran barking after them. There was a smudge mark on the girl's cheek. The sounds from the fete were carried over us and past us into the cor-ridors and sidestreets and dark buildings.

I didnt see your priest, I said.

She shook her head. Then her eyes brightened.

There he is! she said.

A big man sat in a booth with two small children. In the light of two candles I could see his black robes and his red hair. His hand, white and heavy, rested on the head of one of the boys.

Come on, she said. Let's go talk to him.

When he saw us coming, he got to his feet. He was so tall he had to stoop inside the little wooden booth. He patted the children on their heads and then slapped their rumps. The two boys darted past us, giggling. The priest, bent over, peered at us, pulling his nose and clearing his throat. Harrumph! he said. Well, well! He nodded at us and wrung his hands together. Welcome, he said, I'm so glad to see you! How do you like our fete, eh? Come in, sit down! Havent I seen you before? We entered the little cubicle and sat on wooden benches. The priest smiled gleefully. His eyes twinkled in the candlelight. Ah, of course! he said. The bus, the bus, isnt that right? I gave you a little talk, just the other day. I'm so glad you could come!

I live here, I said. She came on the bus.

Ah, of course, said the priest looking carefully at me. That beard. Such an extraordinary thing, eh? You dont often see a beard as colorful as that.

He tugged some more at his nose.

I havent seen you in church either, have I? But no, dont interrupt, let me see if I can guess, youre an atheist, arent you, or an agnostic, which is worse?

Agnostic, I said.

Ah-ha! he cried, and reached over to slap me on the thigh. One can always tell, it's that skeptical look in their eyes! How marvelous! I simply love atheists and agnostics, theyre such stimulating people! Dont you think, my dear?

I didnt know, she said pouting. He's hardly told me a thing about himself, and I've just prattled on and on.

But that's how they are, my dear! Close-mouthed people, they hardly say a word, but you must watch them, yes indeed, theyre clever too, isnt that so? Hah-hah!

He slapped me on the knee again.

Youre a bit clever yourself, I said.

Ho-ho! he said. Flattery!

The girl smiled at him, crossing her legs.

Why is it worse to be an agnostic? she asked.

Ah, my dear, it's quite simple. An atheist has the
courage of his convictions; he rejects outright and takes the
consequences, but the poor agnostic simply stumbles along,
never quite sure which way to go, too cowardly to say no
to God and not brave enough to accept!

Youve got that a bit backward, I said. An agnostic
looks for the truth. He doesnt allow his ignorance to make
him dogmatic.

What did I tell you? said the priest spreading his
hands. He's too clever for an old man like me! But come,
let's discuss more serious things, I'm quite eager to hear
some comments on our fete, or criticisms, if you like. This
is only our first one, but it's going to be an annual affair,
you know, and I want next year's to be even better.

I think it's lovely, the girl said. But it is terribly
crowded. Couldnt you enlarge it a bit, maybe extend it another block, or find an empty lot to have it in?

No, no, my dear, he said. You dont understand these
people, ask your friend here, they love crowds. Theyre so
many of them, all their lives they live in the midst of crowds,
isnt that so, eh? They dont feel comfortable when there's
too much room.

He settled down and crossed his legs; his cloak
opened, and he carefully pinched his trousers and pulled
them up over his knee. The girl sat on the other side of him,
across from me; her small, tanned face had turned serious,
although the beginnings of a smile kept tugging at the corners of her lips. She was small and soft, and the priest was
big but looked soft too: as though, under his black garments,
a boneless body shook with each of his movements. His
eyes were yellowish brown. Outside I could see the two
small children huddled together and giggling. Past the
booth walked people. Their faces were haggard and twisted:
they were dying, they could only limp along and mingle

with the crowds. Two nuns passed, in their swirling robes, well fed and fresh; but they were dying too. The priest grew, the booth was very small; he turned his face to me, his eyes shrewd in the candlelight. He lifted his hand and brought it down on my knee, the fingers gripping tightly. When he opened his mouth I saw his bright teeth and his red tongue.

Well, he said, come on, the agnostic surely has something to say!

I shrugged.

What do you do with the money you make on this fete?

Ah-ha! he said. He looked delightedly from me to the girl. What did I tell you? Right to the heart of the matter. Eh? And where do you think the money goes? Into my pocket, perhaps?

I give up, I said.

A church, he said. What little money we get. Someday we will build a real church, in the middle of this wilderness!

Why not a hospital?

Ah, he said, I see you are a reformer, eh? An idealist! You would change the world with your zeal!

I'm an observer, I said. That's all. Reforming is beyond my power.

And a pessimist too! he said. Such a strange combination!

He patted my knee again, chuckling loudly.

You must make an effort, someday, to understand our position. But now I'm afraid I must leave you. I have my duties to perform, you see. You must come back again some evening, our fete is on all week. Both of you, eh? It's always a pleasure to meet young people—even agnostics and pessimists!

He got to his feet.

Goodnight, my dear, he said to the girl. Keep your eye on him now, wont you?

And still chuckling, he left. The two young children ran up to him, pulling at his robes, and followed him into the crowd. I looked at the girl. Well? I said. She smiled at me, and got to her feet. Why dont we just walk for a while, she said. We went down a sidestreet to avoid the fete. All around us the city was buzzing and muttering. Paper fluttered about in drafts of wind. Shrill melodies hung in the air. It's so lovely at night, she said, gazing upwards at the black sky. The stars were only faint glimmers above us; the air was still full of dust; the light was choked off. A lean black dog raced alongside us for a moment, and then darted into an alley. We walked down a main street, and taxis and trishaws passed us. The drivers slowed down and honked their horns and rang their bells. Taxi, Sahib? Where is Sahib going? One rupee, one rupee only! We shook our heads. The heels on her shoes made clicking noises. During the day, the girl said, the city seems such a desolate place. But at night it all looks cleaner, somehow, nicer, dont you think? It depends, I said, on what part of the city youre in. She nodded thoughtfully. She took my hand. But still I'm glad I came, she said. And I'm glad I met you. Youve no idea how boring those people get, the ones I'm traveling with! She was silent for a moment. Then she asked, Will you be staying here long? I havent really decided, I said. The buildings slowly moved past us. She asked where I was going next, but I told her I didnt know that either. Do you think I'm too forward? she asked. No, I said. She frowned a little at the air. Youre very quiet, she said. Then she stopped and ran to a doorway. Look! she said. Here's a little puppy! She tried to catch it, but the dog darted away from her and ran to an alley, where it stopped and watched us, panting. His thin legs were trembling. Poor little thing! she said. She came back and we walked on, silently. After a while we came to the hotel and stopped at the gates. The ironwork looked cold and sharp.

Would you like to come in for a moment? she asked. No, I said. I'd better not.

We looked at each other.

We're not leaving till Saturday, she said. Perhaps you could come by for tea some afternoon?

I shook my head.

I dont understand you, she said in a soft voice.

Youre a lovely girl, I said.

She smiled a little.

Will you be going to England some day? she asked.

Probably.

She brightened. Let me give you my address, she said. I gave her my pen and she found a scrap of paper. She hurriedly wrote something on it and handed it to me. Here, she said. Really, I'd be delighted to see you. She squeezed my hand. But you really should come by for tea. Perhaps I'll try, I said. I'll look for you, she said. Good night! I opened the gate for her. She waved, and then disappeared into the courtyard. The gate shut with a loud click. The night was purple and black. Down the street I saw the bus, covered in dust and grease. It was spotted with rust, its sides scabrous. The door was open. Inside, the bus would be warm, the air dark. I could see the rows of seats. The fat black tires squatted on the ground. From the windows came the odors of leather and sweat, and the tinkling sounds of voices, stirring in the shadows. As I walked down the road I took the scrap of paper and, without looking at it, tore it into little pieces. For a moment they fluttered alongside me, and then they, too, were gone.

III.

When young I lived in a house on a flat land. My family had lived there for centuries, and that was how our name was derived. I am not proud of it. I have renounced my name. That night I wandered nameless through the city, and no one called out to me, the wind grew, it whistled and chattered, but it did not speak to me. People crossed the street to avoid meeting me. Others lay sleeping on the sidewalks, like bundles of rags, and I stepped over them. Children danced in the road, and trees toppled over. Buildings rose in the midst of ruin. In the end, I told them, it is all the same, the ocean and the sea, the rivers and the streams, the day and the night. The night was full of things, things that moved and twisted, there was blackness everywhere I looked, in the alleys, through the windows, people huddling in the doorways. I crouched there too, and spied on other walkers. I imagined I was in another country; the urge came upon me, and nothing I could do would stop it: to wander, to roam, to walk through the countrysides, to see new faces and new cities and new mountains. But I had been everywhere, I was sure of it. What could I see, now? I had traveled all my life, since I was old enough to leave my father's house. In the end he had let me go, I had become too rebellious to restrain, I refused to work on his land. I argued and fought, I would be free, of all of them. But in the end it was simply another city, another street, another face, and the years faded and twisted them, the colors all ran together. In the end they all died. That was the end of my understanding. I could not go beyond death. In Bombay a Parsee family told me about ghosts, and what this meant, that when we died we still lived on. But I saw no ghosts, and there were too many other explanations for the visions they claimed to see. Holy men preached in tents, and padres too, preachers of all sizes and shapes, but in reality they worshiped the devil they claimed to hate, and he wasnt real either. Their heavens and hells were used only to frighten children, babies in grown up bodies, so the collection plates would tinkle and rustle with money, and the men of god could live in comfort. If that were so, it did not matter where I went. But I followed myself, I could not part with myself. I dragged my body with me, my vision blurred and uncertain. In another country, it was all the same.

The girl who died did not want to die. She screamed at death, but it came anyway. The dust storm raged and bellowed, and when night fastened itself on the land, the teeth clamping into the earth, she was no longer living.

I would like to explain it all, but words lose their meaning. That night I returned at last to my room. The walls became countries, and with my finger I traced my journeys. The son of the family who lived there came in. He sat on my bed while I stared at the wall, following my wanderings. The old woman and the old man were in another room. I could hear her, always rushing about, the old man getting in her way. He would chuckle when she ranted at him and shoved him to one side. The son said nothing, but his silence was meaningful too. His hair was black. He was thin. He brought out his pipe, and together we smoked. The air became tawny and blueish, the walls receded. I imagined I was sitting on a rock overlooking the ocean. The spray came leaping up towards me. Gulls flew in the air, crying. Above, the sky was blue and green, and the ocean was green under my feet, then blue, and in the distance black. I brought her with me, and set her there, so I could see her. The wind blew her hair. Her tanned legs were stretched in front of her. She smiled, a little distantly, her body was taken up by the rocks that trembled at the ocean's assault, by the spray that licked at her face. She was there, but she was part of the rock and the sea.

We argue about small things, I said, things that dont matter.

She turned her head to one side.

Isnt it beautiful here? she said.

In the end, I said, both of us die. We have to learn to live together.

Youre always fighting with me.

I have things I believe in.

But you always tell me you believe in nothing.

It's difficult. It's not that simple.

Why do you need to wander? Youre never satisfied with anything. Why dont you stop, for a while? How long do you think I can go on, like this? You never think of me.

Green moss grew in hollow places in the rocks. Small fish darted about. I hunted for crabs beneath the flat stones.

I'm leaving you, she said. Youve destroyed me, but you wont get any satisfaction out of it.

The ocean in Africa beat against the rocks. Christmas had been spent in Galle, in Ceylon, wandering among the ruins of an old fort. We walked across the ancient walls. The night was spread all around us. Early in the morning, before the sun rose, we took a train further around the island. Then we went by bus to Nurye Elia and Kandy. In Nurye Elia the mist shrouded the mountains, and tea plants grew on the sides of the hills. The bus jerked and bounced, little black streams of water fell down the slopes. The next day we were in Colombo. New Year's Eve disappeared in the firecracker silence of a black night.

In Suva she made coffee, and playfully hissed at the bright blue flames. In Jolo her face blistered and reddened from the sun. Her hair strung around her face, and she gasped for breath. In Olongapo she opened her legs for a sailor, and for three days we ate our tears, for three days she bled with her guilt. In Kota Belud her breasts were soft, she sprawled on a bed, we whispered in the hazy sunshine, but the pain came back in Penang when we huddled in the shadows, comforting each other. I could smell food cooking. I gave her rice. In Dhanashkodi we looked at the wooden shacks. Her frightened face was turned towards the sea. In Nurye Elia the only clothing she wore was the mist, and she almost died from the cold. Droplets of water formed on her body. On the Masai plains, we stared at our haggard faces.

On the Masai plains, the wind blew, and dust rose yellow and red against the sky.

IV.

During the several days that followed, I wandered
all over the city. I even one afternoon found the ocean,
spreading out towards the horizon. I stopped smoking and
drank arak instead. The days were hot and murky, breathing was painful, it was like drawing a file up my throat,
but in the little wooden bars the arak was cool, the alleys
inviting. Sometimes the son went with me, he knew all the
places. Together we walked, we sat in the bars among the
cripples and the beggars and the peasants, the glasses were
filled and tipped. All the time the son asked questions. He
never gave up. Why, he would ask, do you drink arak? Why
do you not go back to your own country, and drink whiskey? Shut up, I'd say, and drink. He never worked, but he
always had a little money. Black market, he explained when
I asked. He knew some people, he had friends all over the
city. Once we went by the hotel. The bus was parked outside, and I saw people moving about in the courtyard. I
thought I could see her hair, blowing in the wind, but I
could not be sure. The son laughed a little, and stared at
me. His eyes were dark and remote; they were always a
little scornful. That is where she is staying? he asked, and I
nodded, although I had told him nothing about her. He
wore long pants, but he was barefoot, his shirt was white
with long tails that flapped in the wind. We stood in the
park. He leaned against a tree, folding his arms, and
watched me. The heat pressed down all around us, but the
air was still, the wind had disappeared. You white men, he
said. You are foolish. A woman is only a woman.

She walked across the courtyard, slender and brown
from the sun. She swam in the ocean, I could see that, she
would love the sea, she swam gracefully and easily. At
night she lay on her bed, one arm thrown out, her legs
curled under her chin. Her breasts were soft and tender.
Between her legs she would be tight and painful, and then
warm and eager. She would blossom out, yielding and

demanding. In the night her body would smell of love. I knew her as well as I knew myself. While I drank arak in the cool bars, I touched her small nipples. She smiled at me in the half light. Love is everything, she said. When you love someone, that is all that matters, everything else will work out. It made me sad, to hear her talk. You are young, I said, and innocent. She pouted. How can I be innocent, she asked, after this? And she smiled slyly. I drank the arak. Next to me sat the son. He played with his glass. Drugs are better, he said. When you drink, all you can do is get drunk. With drugs you can feel almost anything—or nothing. But he drank anyway, to keep me company. The man behind the bar had shifting eyes. He poured the liquor and grinned at everyone, his eyes darting back and forth. On the other side of me sat a young man wearing trousers and shoes; he was a money-changer. He followed the tourists, offering money at the black market rate. Next to him was a beggar in a dirty sarong, nuzzling his glass. He drank slowly. He looked very old, and carried a crutch. After a while two policemen came in, wearing their khaki uniforms, and started drinking.

This country is corrupt, laughed the son, his teeth shining.

Why do you live at home? I asked.

It's cheap, he said. It costs me nothing but patience, putting up with a foolish and stupid mother.

Youre cruel, I said.

Of course. We copy the West. We are liars and thieves and hypocrites. And cruel.

You are determined to be a cynic, I said.

The bar was made entirely of wood; there was no metal or glass; the seats were benches and clumsy stools and the bar at which we sat was only a plank. We were in a single room with two doors, one leading to the street and the other to the alley which was also the urinal. Whenever that door was opened the odors from the alley came into the room. The two big windows facing the street were screened. Few people walked past, there were no cars, only an occasional trishaw passing by. The people who walked were shrouded in white. The trishaws were red and green. The room smelled of arak and sweat, and the few people were either silent or talking in a dialect I did not understand.

But you, of course, said the son, are a Westerner yourself.

Of sorts, I said.

It is rare for a white man to come here. You make the people nervous. They are afraid of you, and they hate you too. But they will call you Sahib if you talk to them.

He sipped at his drink.

This does not annoy you? he asked.

No, I said.

If you were an American, you would want them to love you. If you were British, to respect you, to look up to you. If Australian, to admire you.

What does that make me?

Nothing, he said. Why are you here?

He brushed his hair out of his eyes. I looked away. After a while we left, walking carefully down the street. The buildings rocked over us. The night hovered, ready to fall on our necks. The stars did not exist, they were destroyed by the city. Steam rose from the sidewalks, along with the smell of feces and decaying bodies. Then there were more people on the streets, and we found ourselves among the cages, the buildings older, the alleys running off in all directions. In places there was music; out of some of the windows, on the second stories, girls peered. The son inspected the cages at street level; he knocked on the doors and looked through the holes in the walls. He laughed at some of the women, and nodded at others. Some spat at him, some cursed him, others invited him in, hitching up their saris or dresses. He nudged me, he took my arm and led me to the doorways. My friend, he said. You like my friend? Finally I pushed him into one of the rooms, and shut the door behind him. When he came out he was dark in the face and his eyes were flashing. Youre embarrassed, I told him. Youre embarrassed and angry. Dont tell me you are a cynic—youre a boy. He remained sullenly at my side. I spit on you, he said at last. I spit on all of your people.

But he did not move, and in a few minutes he laughed. You are a strange man, he said. You are very quiet. You do not waste your words. We came to the steps of the whorehouse. The wood was unpainted and splintering. In the room at street level a woman stared at us. When we looked in her direction, she smiled. She had no teeth, and her face was scarred; her black hair was a tangled mass falling to her waist. She held her hands out to us, her nails long but un-cared for, her palms darkly lined. Her eyes were very hot. I led the way up the stairs, into the coolness. Around the table, on sofas and a few chairs, sat the women, twelve of them. Frowning and smiling, they waited for us. They giggled and shuffled their feet and stared at the air in front of them. There were no roses in vases, the vases had disappeared, but there was a shining mirror on the wall. The small girl grinned at me. She patted her hands on her knees. The son and I sat down, and I ordered a beer, and the mama relayed the command without getting to her feet. She sank into her own flesh. The beer was green and frothy, but I paid the three rupees. The son asked me if I came here for a woman. No, I said, I came here for the beer. He grinned, appraising the women. His white teeth flashed in the dark air. The long-legged woman, wearing tight pants and high heels, got to her feet and went to the mirror. She inspected her lipstick and touched her hair with her fingers. She went back to her seat, brought out a cigarette, and smoked. The small girl smiled whenever I looked in her direction. She bounced a little, ready to jump up from her seat. The young man laughed. I want to see which one you pick, he said. Then I must go. I do not pay for my women. I gave the mama the money and stood up. Good-bye, I said to him. The small girl met me, and we went to her room. The son got up, laughing without making a sound, and then I shut the door.

You come back to me, no? she said. Your ship do not leave?

No ship, I said. I live here.

Ah. She smiled up at me. Then you come here often, yes? I very good for you. You remember, eh?

I promise, I said to myself, I promise to remember everything. I promise to forget nothing. I lay down on the bed, and she knelt beside me, putting her hand on my groin. She let her dress fall into her lap, and with a quick movement her brassiere came open. Her brown breasts moved over my face. You like me, no? she said. That is why you come back? That is why, I said to myself. The room was small, the sheets on the bed were gray. Her tiny hands unbuttoned my pants, and pulled them off. On the floor a pan held gray water. You want me suck you? she said. She put my penis in her mouth and pulled at it, at the same time pushing her dress past her legs. It fell to the floor and lay there without moving. All the time I could hear noises in the building, not people, but the trembling of the wood, the boards creaking together, the house muttered and groaned, little drafts of wind came stealthily into the room, tip-toeing over the floor, they curled along my legs, and I felt cold air on my chest. The girl's buttocks were in the air, and her mouth working. I could smell the spices of her body as she became warmer and drops of sweat appeared on her back. She still wore her panties, and I could see the cleft between her buttocks. Her breasts swung back and forth. She took her mouth away and pressed a breast into my groin. Ugh, she grunted. You lazy man, make me do all work. She pulled off her panties. They lay on the floor, grayish white, slowly collapsing. Somewhere in the house music started. The girl turned around, facing me, and squatted so I entered into her. First she was tight and dry, and it was painful; then she loosened and became damp. As she moved, the music whimpered and wailed, and the pan of water on the floor vibrated. I shut my eyes. Her face was smiling at me, her eyes bright, but I wanted to listen to things: the house as it shifted minutely, the night as it pressed onto the earth, my heart beating in my chest. When it was finished, the girl got off and lay beside me.

It is strange, I said. I am afraid of heights, and so I have climbed mountains. I am afraid of water, so I swim in the ocean. I am afraid of new places, places where I am a stranger, and so I have always traveled. I am afraid of women, so I fuck everything I find. And I am afraid of death. What should I do about that?

I do not know what you say, she said sweating beside me.

I am afraid of death. But is it logical to kill myself? Should I kill myself to prove my courage is greater than my fear?

I do not know what you say, she said. You do not talk about such thing. You come back to me, so I make you feel better. But you do not be so lazy. It is very hard for me. Okay?

The next day I watched the bus leave. It filled up with people, and I even saw her: she wore a yellow dress and her hair was tied in a bun. Everyone got on the bus and the engine started up. Black smoke came from the exhaust. People gathered around to watch, and I could see the faces of the passengers in the row of windows. The palm trees rustled in the wind. The sky was pale blue. The bus coughed and groaned, the motor roared, the metal sides and cowlings trembled, and it started on its way. Little whiffs of dust followed it. People parted before it. It gathered speed, leaning forward, snarling at the crowds. The bus sped around a corner, still blowing black smoke, and disappeared. It was a very warm day.

PART THREE

I.

I am confused by the purple mountains in my memory. I am confused by the woman who lies on my bed, dead after so many years of suffering, her skin turned purplish by the twilight. I am confused, also, by the people who appear in my memory, and this is strange: all my life I have been proud of my knowledge of others. I had only to look at them to understand them, men, women, children, it did not matter, from the look in their eyes, from the way they walked or the words they chose, I could see through them. They became transparent to me. Nor did it matter whether they were whites or Malays or Indians or Moros or even Chinese. I met them in Bangkok and Shiasi, Wandagee and Penang, Kota Belud and others, thousands of places. But I no longer understand things; they have slipped from my grasp. I remember only faces and villages, the cities full of streets, the monsoon clouds coming low over the hills.

The trishaw driver does not talk to me, not really. He only answers my questions and calls me Sahib. Sometimes he smiles. A long time ago I gave him some money and told him to drive me through the city: it was too hot to walk. But the heat was hurting him, too. He had shriveled and dried; his face was full of creases; the skin on his arms and legs was splotched, as though with rust. He could hardly speak, he gasped his words out. When he took the money his hands trembled, his mouth opened and closed as he breathed, his tongue and lips black. He pedaled slowly, sunk over the handlebars, his white sarong tucked around his waist, leaving his legs free. Sometimes he turned to look at me, pleading with eyes the color of worms: he was going blind. I sat upright in my cushioned seat. To the cages, I told him. We will start our tour at the cages. Obediently, he pedaled down the streets. Around me was a sea of brown faces, the sun burnt through the sky, the heat rose in my throat. Dust from the road, composed of dirt and manure, lifted into the air. Men were spitting and coughing, a naked child rubbed his groin with a tiny fist. A sari-wrapped woman picked her nose, and between her legs I saw the legs of a child, endlessly fidgeting. When we reached the cages I told the trishaw driver to stop. It was the middle of the afternoon, but the streets were still busy. I leaned back for a moment and watched the traffic, bullock carts and dogs and stray men. Passing me, calling in shrill voices, were peddlers and hawkers, carrying trays of food and trinkets, curries and fish, bronze gods and colored movie stars.

Hey there, one cried out, are you still selling last week's fish?

Hi-yah! Hi-yah! another shouted, waving statues in the air.

Hey, old man, you had better sell some of that load before it crushes you!

Some of them pranced and scampered, others dragged their feet, and always shooting past them were tinkling trishaws and roaring buses. People darted back and forth. Women huddled in doorways, their shawls clenched tight around their bodies.

I heard a clanking and rattling noise, and looked up. The sound came from one of the whorehouses, and was followed by a shrill cry, and then the babble of women screaming over each other's voices. The trishaw driver nervously looked at me; his mouth was open, and his tongue swollen up, pressing against his black teeth. The people crouched on the sidewalk didnt move. Perhaps the heat was too much, the exertion would be too painful. Down the stairway of one of the houses near me, clattering onto the street, came a metal crutch. It hit a beggar on the leg, but perhaps he didnt notice it, the beggar didnt stir, sitting with the one leg stretched before him. Then came another crutch; it too clattered and banged as it came down the stairs. There was a loud, painful shout, and then the house was silent. The trishaw driver started to peddle onward, but I stopped him. The buses rushed past us. People darted back and forth, and others crouched silent. Coming down the stairway I saw a leg and a hand: the hand lifted the leg and moved it forward. A small child peered up, and then ran away. Descending the stairs on his rump, lifting and shoving his legs forward, came a short plump man, dressed as a European, complete with shoes and socks. His pant legs were pulled up, and his legs were white. When he reached the bottom of the stairs, he bent his head forward, like a bird; his mouth was trembling and spittle clung to his lips; his hair shone like a fire, a red fire on top of a white and puffy face. One short, plump arm reached forward and grasped a crutch, then he wiggled forward to reach the other.

Sahib, said the trishaw driver plaintively.

Wait, I said.

The crutches fitted his hands and straps went around his arms as high as his elbows. He juggled with the crutches and then got trembling to his feet. Standing, he was a terrible figure. His back was broad, his hips wide; his belly was pregnant; he leaned forward, dripping spittle; tiny red eyes darted up and down the street. Very slowly he breathed. I watched his chest fill with his breath, and then collapse, and fill again. There were sweat stains under his arms. His face was colorless, and his arms too, his lips without blood. As an empty trishaw passed, he raised his crutch and shook it, and made a shouting sound. The driver of the trishaw rose off his seat, and hurried by, tinkling his bell at the people in front of him. Slowly the cripple's eyes passed up and down the street. The people sitting near him became smaller. Children hid beneath their mothers, and the women turned their eyes away, saying prayers.

He looked at me, and breathed. His chest went in and out. The red eyes fastened on me. He wiped his lips and swung himself unsteadily towards me.

Sahib, pleaded the trishaw driver.

Excuse me, the cripple said. His eyes flickered and his voice had become quiet. Yours seems to be the only trishaw here. Perhaps you are going my way?

I'm not going any way in particular, I said. I'll be pleased to take you wherever you like.

He grunted, and with quick practiced movements unhooked his crutches and threw them on the seat next to me, leaning against the carriage as he did so. His legs bowed and trembled. Do you want any help? I asked. I'm a cripple, he said with a snarl in his voice, I am not incompetent. The trishaw rocked and swayed, and then he was sitting beside me, gathering up his crutches. The trishaw driver stared at us unhappily. Sahib, he said, it is very hot, and I am very old man. The cripple shook a crutch at him. Get on with you! he said. Lazy bugger! Straight ahead! He turned to me. His body smelled of sweat, sour and damp. Filthy swines, he said. Uncivilized. As bad as the country they live in. You are American, are you not?

How do you guess? I asked.

He grunted. He blew air through his mouth, his cheeks puffed up.

I am an expert, he said. I am an expert in languages. I am a professional man. You need only say a few words, and I know.

He became silent, and we passed through the city. In the heat, the sweat poured off him, and his smell became terrible. Like acid, it ate into me, and I felt myself shrink and burn. Away from the cages the streets became almost empty: here people would appear only in the cool of the evening, and I saw only a few beggars, blind men and men without legs, squatting in the sun. A few women clung to shadowed walls; children lay about, panting. I leaned back and shut my eyes, I smiled at the empty space in front of me, at the trishaw driver, at the cripple beside me. He spoke only to give directions. My red skin shone in the sunlight, my beard yellow. We crossed streams smelling of urine and shit and the dead bodies which lay there, slowly coming apart, eaten by worms and covered with flies. The trishaw driver pedaled slowly. When we came to a hill, it was only by straining, putting what weight he had on the pedals, that we could move. I opened my eyes: his thin figure twisted and coiled with effort, yet we barely made headway. It is hard, I said, for the trishaw driver. The cripple grunted. Bah! he said. He is only a beast. Let him go. He puffed his cheeks and blew air through his mouth.

Youre an albino, arent you, I said.

He grunted again and rattled his crutches at the trishaw driver.

Get on with you! he said. Lazy bugger!

Yes, he said to me. Of course. I am an albino. I am crippled because of an operation on my brain, two years ago. A tumor. I am a countryman of that—he waved a crutch—filthy beast. Is there anything else you wish to know?

He settled back into his seat. His arms shook, and when he handled his crutches they rattled. With a last burst of effort the trishaw driver carried us over the hill, and as we started down, coasting, he slumped over the handlebars. I could see his thin belly heaving. We had left the main part of town, with its two and three story buildings, and all the structures around us now were made of wood, hardly more than shacks, with signs in Hindi lettering over the shops. The people wore rags and stared at us. They were

dirty and thin. Cattle roamed the streets, switching their
tails at the flies. Ahead of us, white and shining, was a single
concrete building, flat and low. As we drew up to it, I saw
it held mostly government offices: the Department of Agri-
culture, the Department of Health, and the Bureau of Pub-
lic Welfare. Lying in front of the doorways were sleeping
people. At the end of the building was another door with a
red rooster over it; its windows were curtained. We stopped
in front of it.

Do you work here? I asked.

No.

For a moment he fidgeted with his crutches. His
eyes flickered at me and darted away.

Would you like a drink? he suddenly asked.

Certainly, I said. Is this a bar?

He said nothing, but slung himself off the carriage,
rocking the trishaw so it almost tipped over. He slipped his
crutches on and went to the driver. Here, I told him, wait a
moment, I'll pay him, it was I who hired him. The cripple
turned to glare at me. Do you think I am unable to pay? he
snarled. His hand darted into his pocket, and came up with
bills. He gave the driver a rupee and a few coins. I'll give
him another rupee, I said. It was a hard trip. The trishaw
driver looked at me gratefully. No, said the cripple harshly,
dont be foolish, youll corrupt him. I know these people,
they would rob their own mother. The driver tried to say
something, but a crutch was waved in his face. Get on, now!
said the cripple. Out of our way! The driver slumped over
the handlebars, his arms hanging loosely. The cripple swung
around him and led me to the dark doorway. He halted
there a moment. He breathed slowly, evenly, and wiped
his face. His eyes constantly jerked back and forth, but he
seemed to make an effort to control them, gathering himself. He propped one crutch against the door and brushed
at his clothes, tucking in his shirt. All right, he said to me,
come. His voice was low and quiet. He swung open the
door and we entered.

Immediately I felt darkness fluttering at my face; as the door closed behind me, darkness came swooping in, patting at my cheeks and arranging my shirt. At the same time, from a corner of the room, a silk dress rustled and two thin arms stretched forward. Within the dress was a tiny creature with long hair, she swept towards us, a smile in her eyes. The cripple standing next to me was grinning; his face became red with pleasure. In the background a little music stirred, and on the tables were candles: their flames wavered as the girl moved past them, and shadows rushed back and forth across the walls. Welcome! she cried in a voice as small as she was. Hello, hello! It's good to see you again! The cripple bowed and nodded his head. His teeth glittered. She took his arm and looked brightly towards me. The cripple unhooked one hand and gestured in my direction. A friend, he said, I b-brought a friend. It was the first time I had heard him stutter. Oh, how do you do, she said, it's good to meet you! She gave me a small and limp hand. I squeezed it and gave it back. Please, she said, come and sit down. She led us to a table and saw we were seated. What can I bring you? she asked. The first drink for a stranger is free, she said to me. I tried to say something, but she raised a hand. No, no! she said. It is a custom of the house, one of my little customs! We have anything you like, whiskey, gin, beer, even arak! Have you tried arak already? I nodded. Oooh, terrible, isnt it? she said. As bad as whiskey! In that case, I said, I'll have gin, with tonic perhaps. She turned to the cripple. And the professor? she asked. The same as always? He nodded his head happily, and she turned away, her dress swinging and shimmering. I looked around. We were the only customers.

It is early, said the cripple. The people do not come until later.

I nodded.

And are you a professor? I asked.

No, no, he said, waving a hand. It is merely one of her fictions. I was at the university before, but I was not a professor.

And now? I asked.

And now, he said (fists trembling on the table, eyes staring down), and now I am an assistant in a government office for the study of language.

The girl returned with our drinks. My eyes were now adjusted to the darkness, and on her forehead I saw a red, tear-shaped beauty mark; her black hair, shining and long, was tightly combed back, falling over one shoulder. Her face was small and fine. She directed a smile at me.

You are in our country long? she asked.

A few weeks, I answered.

Ah, yes, she said, and how do you find it? It is such a dirty place, dont you think? It must be different in your country, very beautiful. I am so sick of this country, and this city, it is so filthy. That is why I almost never leave my little place, the Red Rooster! She tossed her head back and laughed. It is a beautiful name, no, the Red Rooster? Do you know why I call it that? Because when my friends come here, they are always crowing! Like roosters, they are always crowing and bragging! Except for the professor, she said placing a hand on his arm (smiling, he looked at her tiny fingers). The professor is always so quiet! Did you know that he is our people's leading expert in languages?

Is he? I said.

But yes! In all of our country, there is no one like him! And it is so terrible, about the operation, and what the university did.

She cocked her head to one side and looked sadly at the cripple. He was grinning, looking down at the table top.

And he was such a popular man, she said. Always ladies around him!

Heh-heh! he chuckled.

It was because of his white skin, she said, and because he was so clever!

He raised his head and frowned.

And now! he said.

Yes, she sighed, and now they will not look at him! We women are so fickle!

Even the whores, he said bitterly.

Even the whores, she said. It is so sad.

What did the university do? I asked.

He blew angrily across the table, his cheeks puffed out.

They kicked me out! he said.

Yes! she said. They kicked him out! Now they will not let him teach, even study!

Now I am an—assistant!

Yes, she said. A man of his ability, an assistant!

She made a clucking noise with her tongue.

I do not know what to do, he said.

I bring you another drink, she said.

She brought us fresh glasses.

Do you know, said the cripple smiling again, she is one of our best poets?

A poet? I said.

No, no, she laughed. I have not written a poem for years! Soon it will be five years, no? So terrible!

She has had her poems, said the cripple, in all of our best papers.

What are your poems about? I asked.

Oh, she said, blood!

Blood?

Yes, she said. Always blood! I cannot write a poem without blood in it! I think I must have a fixation, no? So much blood!

And your friends who come here, I said, they are poets also?

Yes, she said, poets and authors. That is why I call my place the Red Rooster, because they are always crowing about it!

We drank. Soon a man and a woman came in, both dressed in the European style, and she leaped up to greet them. Welcome! she cried. Hello, hello! It's good to see you again! They were seated at another table, and she sat with them. The cripple and I drank, quietly. The room became noisier and smaller, and the darkness was filled with shadows. The couple and the girl were talking about poetry. So much blood! I heard her say. So terrible!

II.

I could feel myself slowly fill up with liquor. I could feel my face turning red, and the cripple's too, red in the flare of our candle. The drinks were ruby-colored, and a ring on the cripple's finger was shining like a red sunset. There was so much redness, everywhere; it was like a desert in another land, where the red barren earth spread all around me; the red sand caught and twisted at my feet; I was alone, walking across the desert; at each rock I stumbled; at each drift I felt the sand clinging at my ankles; I could only slog forward, as though going through a swamp. The earth turned, and the sunset became a sunrise: the sun went down in the west, and rose again in the east. All the time I walked. It was an endless procession. I set it to music, and sang as I struggled along. All my life, I sang to myself, I have walked across the red desert. My voice was dry and harsh. All my life, I sang to myself, walking has been difficult, even standing upright: the sun nesting in my hair, like a warm bird. The weight was forcing me down. Yet if I lowered my head I would die. Behind me floated death, effortless on the wind. When the breeze stirred, I could feel him pressing down on me. His eyes and skin were red, but his shadow was black. I will not lower my head, I sang, always I will march upright, my head straight. But I did not fool him. In this room, I thought, he hides in the corners, he peers at me from behind the cripple's eyes. His hand was heavy on his glass. He lifted it with effort, slowly, his muscles straining. His eyes became wet and shiny. My body shone with sweat, the sun had turned me red, my hair almost white. In the end, the red sun would wear me away. The cripple stared at me. His thin lips glittered.

I'm going outside for a minute, I told him.

He only grinned at me, nodding his head.

Night had fallen, but outside it was still warmer than inside the bar. The night was purple and blue, and tiny white stars were flickering overhead. People were still sleeping in front of the other offices. They did not move, the people, they did not make a sound. They were only bundles of rags with faces and flat, dark feet. The trishaw driver was sprawled over his handlebars. He turned his face to look at me, and I smiled at him. I trod lightly over the earth. If each step, I thought, were a hundred miles. Ten steps would be a thousand. Over the land I would stride, a giant. But I did not stride, I tip-toed, I carefully passed around the building to its rear. An alley was there, it ran straight and narrow between the white (though stained) concrete and a collection of wooden walls. The darkness in there was complete, the faint light from the stars could not penetrate it. I stood there for a moment, swaying. From the darkness came the odors of things dead and half-dead, of garbage and tin cans and rotting carcasses. The air lay on the ground without moving. I stepped into it, keeping my hand on the wall. After a short distance I stopped, opened my pants, and urinated. The yellow liquid was warm, I could hear it spatter and steam, joining the other odors. When I turned I stepped on something soft and slippery. My arms threshing the air did no good. I reflected on it, sadly, as I fell, but at the last moment I drew my arms and legs in, pulled my head into my shoulders, and sat.

I'm sorry, I said when I had regained my breath.

Quite all right, a voice sighed.

I sat there, breathing. The ground was hard and lumpy. Soon the darkness lifted slightly, and I saw the man. He lay just before me, his legs apart, naked. There were gray worms crawling violently over and in his belly.

Youre sure I didnt hurt you? I asked.

Not at all, he said in a soft voice. No one can hurt me now.

How did you happen to come here?

He didnt move, but I could sense his shoulders trying to shrug.

Where else? he said.

True, I answered. It doesnt much matter, I suppose.

We were silent for a few minutes; but the silence became oppressive. I could feel the black sky hanging over my head.

It's warm, I said.

Yes, it's always warm.

Have you been here long?

Three days, I think, he said painfully. I think it is three days.

Three days!

Perhaps four. Yes, I think perhaps it is four, now. It's not easy to remember.

You are waiting for something.

Yes, he said. I am waiting.

We were silent again, but it was difficult sitting there. There were worms on my foot. I looked at them with surprise. I picked up a stick and brushed them off. They rapidly crawled over the ground back to the man. Uneasily, I stared around. I could see nothing but the man, the ground between us, my foot, and the suggestion of the walls on either side of us. The concrete wall appeared faintly gray, the other side was darker.

Is there something I can do for you? I asked.

Perhaps you could keep me company, he said. For a short time. I'm sure the cart will be here soon.

Gladly. What cart is that?

The dead cart.

It must be unpleasant.

You have no conception.

Instead of eyes, he had two clusters of flies on his face. They were iridescent, blue and black and green. They seemed to turn in my direction.

What about the girl? he suddenly asked in a sly tone of voice.

Immediately it became black, and I could no longer see him. I stared in the direction he had been.

What girl? I asked. What girl are you talking about?

But he did not answer. The blackness was silent, the walls had disappeared, even my foot. I stirred, so I could feel my body. I was very heavy; I discovered my arms were sore and stiff, burning from the heat of the day; the sun had coated me with soreness. The heat slowly eased from my body, burning my skin as it left. I tried to stand up, but my head was wobbling too badly. I have drunk too much, I said to myself. It is simply that. I drink, and I can no longer control my head, or even my eyes. The black night pressed down on me. Cautiously I felt around with my hand.

Where are you? I asked. Where have you gone?

I'm here, he said. I'm always here.

I saw him again. Now he was sitting against the white wall, his legs crookedly in front of him. His head had fallen forward, and his jaw had dropped onto his chest. The mouth was wide open, and I saw flies buzzing around inside it. They sparkled and shone, darting back and forth over his half-eaten tongue.

I thought you had gone, I said.

Gone? he mocked. Gone? I, gone?

I wasnt sure, I couldnt see you.

He laughed shortly, and flies flew from his mouth. Then he coughed, a dry, ragged sound, coming from deep within his chest. But his chest did not move, nor his throat, his jaw, or his eyes. There was only the cough, bitterly rasping, and a small cloud of flies darting about in front of him. When the cough stopped, they all returned to his mouth.

I'm sorry, he said. I shouldnt laugh. It is not something to laugh about.

I moved uncomfortably.

I wish there were more light, I said.

No, no more light. It is bad enough, in the dark. I was never proud of my appearance, but now—I am glad I cannot see.

How can you tell it is dark?

I can tell that. I can tell the dark from the light. I even know where you are sitting. But I cannot see.

And during the day? I asked. What do you do then?

Nothing, he said. I just sit here, waiting for the dead cart. Sometimes I listen to the people. I can hear them talking, and moving about. To pass the time I make a game of it—wondering which of them will be next.

How unpleasant!

Yes, but I am in an unpleasant situation. There is a child, in one of the buildings here. I think he will be next. He wont last the night. But he'll be buried, perhaps, and wont have to wait. Not like me—waiting for the dead cart. He screamed a lot yesterday, but today he was quiet. A while ago an old woman was wailing. Did you hear it?

No, I said. I was in the bar, behind you.

Yes, of course. There's an old man, too—or perhaps not so old, I cannot tell. He came here last night to relieve himself, as you did. His piles were like yellow mucous. They glittered in the starlight very beautifully. But he grunted and cried while he squatted, not far from where you are, he cried and sobbed with the pain of relieving himself. Perhaps he'll die before the child. And then there's you, of course.

I shook my head.

No, I said, youre mistaken, I'm quite healthy, I havent been sick for years!

Please, he said. I have no doubt youll survive the
night. I didnt mean to frighten you. But your life is so short,
you know. Time—it runs on. There's no turning back. It
doesnt matter what road you take. Someday, before youre
quite ready for it, youll meet me again.

I looked away. For a moment I thought I could hear
a woman wailing.

We all have to die, I said.

Yes, that's quite a comfort.

How do you mean? I asked sharply. How can it be
a comfort?

Please, he said. Youre getting excited again. It's so
uncomfortable here. If only I could move a bit—but I'm
dreaming again. No, I only meant that when someone
dies—particularly if one had a hand in it—you can comfort yourself by saying that. That everyone has to die.

What are you trying to say? I said. Youre getting at
something, youre trying to dig at me.

No, no, he said sighing again. You take everything
too personally. It's easy to see you feel guilty. But I didnt
mean anything. I even apologize for mentioning the girl.
You see? I mean no harm, not I.

Youre quite wrong, I said. I dont feel guilty at all.
There was nothing I could do. There was a dust storm,
you see, for three days there was a dust storm, so there
was no traffic. What would you have me do? Carry her?
For a hundred miles? There was nothing I could do, nothing at all.

But he laughed again, and then choked. The dry
rasping cough dragged up through his chest, and the flies
clouded about in front of his mouth. When at last he
stopped, the flies returned. They sparkled blue and black
and green against his tongue.

You see what youve done? he complained. Youve
made me laugh again. Ah, if only the dead cart would come!
Peace! Silence! An end to it!

After a moment he chuckled.

What am I saying? he asked. An end to it! I've already arrived at the end!

I loved her, I said. That's why I made her come with me.

Yes, yes, he said. I'm sure. But I wont mention her again. I can see it upsets you. Is that a bell I hear?

I dont hear anything.

Perhaps not. One always hears what one wants to hear. Still, I'm sure it will come tonight. But listen!

He was quiet for a moment.

There! Do you hear it? Do you hear it now?

Far off in the night came a tinkling sound.

Yes, I said. I hear something—little bells.

Ah, he sighed. At last. Soon it will be here. Unless they miss me. You dont think theyll miss me, do you?

I dont know, I said. It's something I know nothing about.

Perhaps, when they come closer—

I'm sure theyll find you, I said.

Yes, of course, youre right. They always look here. People like this place. Every few days, someone comes here to die. Why, I remember one week, they took eight bodies from this alley. In one week, mind you! There is a sort of history to this place. It comforts me to think about it. Dogs, too, animals, not just men. Women and children. There is something—attractive about this place.

The bells tinkled again, a little closer.

See here, he said, you do forgive me, dont you? I mean, for mentioning her. I meant no harm, really. And youre right, of course, in the end everyone has to die. But tell me—was she pretty?

I dont have to sit here, I said. I dont have to sit here and listen to you.

But I didnt move.

Of course, he said. I've offended you again. Yet I have the best intentions. Only the best, I assure you.

I'm going to leave, I said. I wont listen to you.

Perhaps youre right. Youre right to leave. Really, I'm incorrigible. There's no telling what I'll say next, I'm not a responsible person. But on the way out, perhaps you could call out to the dead cart? Let them know there's a—customer—for them here? Could you do that, when you leave?

I didnt move. He laughed, and started coughing again. Between the fits he choked out: There, youve done it again! —All this laughing!—No good at all!—Your fault!—Making me laugh like this!—Peace!—Peace! Then he was silent, and the flies returned to his mouth, buzzing and moving about. The bells tinkled again, more loudly, and I heard someone shout, and a few voices in the distance.

Ah, he said, theyve stopped. Someone stopped the dead cart. I wonder who it was. Who the—customer was. Perhaps I knew him. But it's hard to keep up, I cant tell you how hard. They die so fast. Here one moment, gone the next. Ah—I nearly laughed again! Peace, peace!

The bells started tinkling again, and rapidly drew nearer. The man seemed to be listening, he didnt say a word, and even the flies stopped their whirring and buzzing. After a moment he started talking, but more to himself than me: I wonder who will be on the cart tonight. Will there be anyone I know? Men and women, a few children, I'm sure, beggars and cripples, that's who they get, people with no family, none to care for them. Have they much further to go? Or will it be a long trip yet, up and down these streets? I'm sure the cart will jog and bounce quite a bit; these roads arent what they should be. Everyone packed in, lying on top of each other, guts and blood and what have you. Altogether unpleasant, I should imagine, though that doesnt matter much any more. But then he stopped again; we heard the steady clop of the bullocks pulling the cart, and the creak of the wheels; the tinkling bells were loud and discordant. One would imagine, he sighed to himself, that they could make the music more melodious—though I suppose that racket is only fitting, and after all, it doesnt announce anything too pleasant, does it? A shadow stopped in front of the alley, and the bells and the clop of bullock feet ended. The moon must have emerged from behind some cloud, or perhaps the stars had brightened: the alley glowed with a new light. I could see now the litter on the ground, the old clumps of feces, bones from dogs and cats and other animals, perhaps men too; broken bottles and tin cans with ragged edges, splintered crates of wood, scraps of paper and cardboard. It all lay there, lifeless and unmoving. Two shadows separated themselves from the dead cart; they crunched over the uneven ground, and I could hear their short harsh breaths. When they drew near I could even make out their features. One was tall and stooped, his bare legs were corded with muscles, his long arms swung at his sides. The other was short and broad; he had a dark and scarred face. Neither paid any attention to me. They came up to the dead man and produced metal hooks. The hooks were dull, perhaps rusted steel, or bronze corroded and dark. The tall man took his hook and inserted it under the dead man's jaw, its blade pointing up into the cranium. The short man slid his into the groin, turning it to one side so it caught at the pelvis. All the flies left the dead man; for a moment they buzzed in the air in a little cloud, shining in the light, sparkling green and black and even red, then they flew off, all in different directions. As the dead man was dragged away, he spoke to me once more: None too gentle, are they? he said in a faint voice. Not at all, not gentle at all. None of them on the dead cart can be called gentle, this sort of work takes the gentleness out of you. He was dragged to the mouth of the alley. Still, he said in a voice so faint I could barely make it out, one cant expect more, really; one can expect so little of anyone, anytime. His body was heaved into the air with a grunt by the two men.

The weight disappeared from my shoulders. I got to my feet and carefully picked my way over the rubbish. The dead cart started moving again, although neither the tall nor the short man said a word. The bullocks were black, misshapen beasts, their horns sawed off short. The cart itself was made from saplings, young trees cut down before they had a chance to really grow. Inside it I could see the bodies, one after another, tiers of them, legs and arms hanging out between the poles, even an occasional head. The bells were hung all along its side, and the swaying and jarring motion set them to life. The cart went around to the front of the building. The trishaw driver was staring at the cart in horror, his eyes were wide open, he was sitting bolt upright on his seat. The cart stopped, and one of the men got down and went to the bodies in front of the doorways. He nudged them, one by one. The sleeping people awoke, grunting and moaning, but one remained silent no matter how much he was prodded and tugged. He was dragged away from the others, who were going back to sleep. The tall man went through the clothes, and found nothing, but the short man took off the shirt and put it on his seat on the cart. They inserted their hooks—a little blood came out, perhaps a moan—and threw the body on top of the others. They wiped their hands. Their clothes were greasy. The bullocks stood there, black lumps of muscle and flesh. Then they started again, without giving me a glance, tinkling down the street. The arms and legs and heads in the cart jogged up and down, the cart swayed to and fro, the wheels clanked and bumped over the road. The bodies shifted, bounced and swayed. The cart bounced and clattered, the many bells tinkled, at odds with each other, a discordant melody passing down the street.

III.

I watched the silence gather round. It came nuzzling up to me on the night breeze, rubbing against my cheek. The sleeping bodies lay unmoving and quiet; perhaps in their sleep they did not breathe, they were only bundles of clothes, ankles, feet, hands and heads, curled and sprawled before the doorways. The trishaw driver was still sitting upright and staring in front of him, gripping the handlebars. The tinkling bells faded away into the distance. I opened the door of the Red Rooster and went inside.

It was darker inside than out, but I could see the cripple. He was standing uncertainly on his crutches, his head hanging forward, nodding slightly. The girl in the silk dress was standing next to him, her arm out. For a moment the cripple looked at me, blinking his eyes, as though he did not recognize me. Then the girl cried: Oh, hello! We thought you had left! I shook my head. No, I said, as you can see—I was just getting some fresh air, the drinks were going to my head. Youre leaving? I asked the cripple. He continued to stare at me, blinking his red eyes. His arms trembled on his crutches, and his head nodded up and down, sleepily. Then he straightened himself, and his eyes focused on me. Yes, he said, his voice meek, absent. A ride. I thought perhaps—the air is cooler now. He turned to the girl and smiled, his face shining. The drinks, I think, are going to my head also. She smiled in return, patting his arm. It is good for you, no? she said. That is what I always believe. But that is what I have to believe, isnt it? Otherwise I would be a hypocrite, as well as a poet who does not write! The cripple grinned, letting his head continue to nod, and turned to me. You would like to ac-accompany me? he asked. We went out the door together. The girl shook my hand again and patted the cripple some more on the arm. Outside the trishaw driver had once again slumped over his handlebars. The sky was dark blue. The trishaw driver's clothes were white and covered with stains. The dark, wooden buildings looked ready to collapse, the merest tremor would demolish them.

The trishaw driver was awakened with a shout; he came upright, staring about wildly, and started to protest. The cripple cut him off, waving a crutch in front of his face, and we climbed on board. The old man pedaled slowly down the street, his body rising and straining. The cripple

was quiet; he seemed almost asleep; his head had fallen
forward, and nodded with the motion of the trishaw. The
buildings slowly passed us. There were few creatures moving about, only an occasional dog or beggar, but men and
women and even children were sprawled everywhere,
sleeping. They cluttered the alleys and the doorways. Then
the cripple looked at me sideways, his eyes red.

I thought we could go to the park, he said softly.
The night air—it's pleasant outside.

I shrugged.

You mean, I said, if the prostitutes wont have you,
perhaps the queers will?

He scowled; but after a moment he chuckled.

You are right, he said. What can one do? A man is
not like a woman. He must have sex, or he is not a man, eh?

He shouted at the trishaw driver to hurry, but the
old man could not pedal any faster. The buildings slowly
moved past us, dark and silent.

You are right, he said again. I can no longer have a
woman, unless I pay a fortune. Filthy whores! Once they
would have stood in line for me, yes, they would. I have
traveled, too—before this! There were women everywhere.
My friends were jealous, all of them. No one was as suc-
cessful with the women as I. It was because of my white
skin and my education—I could flatter them, twist them
around my finger! Yes, everywhere I went, Delhi and
Bombay and Karachi, the women came to me! You find that
hard to believe, eh? Looking at me now?

No, I said, it's quite possible.

He chuckled and took the crutches in his hand. For
a moment he stared at them, shaking them a little.

So low have I come! he said loudly. So complete my
descent!

He rattled the crutches, and then continued softly.

A descent into hell. My friends have deserted me,
the university will not have me. The women are gone. You
think I exaggerate, eh? Exaggerate my little hell? But you

are foolish. You are a Westerner, an American, in fact, well fed, pampered, and rich. What can you know? he said bitterly; spittle appeared in little white flakes on his lips. My life is over. I only exist. What can I look forward to? The filthy mouth of a homosexual! The asshole of a queer! Yes, that is all. People avoid me. Who wants to be seen with a man like me? Children cry when I come close. Children of my countrymen, beggars in the streets! I am hidden away in a little office. Some day it must end. Some day I will end it. When there is nothing to live for, a man must die.

In the still air the sweat of his body was powerful and acidic. In the still night air his voice had taken on a doglike whine, and in the distance, from the alleys, the far streets, I heard dogs howling and crying. Yellow pups with ticks on their legs staggered by. A thin black dog trotted alongside for a moment, his head lowered, his red tongue almost dragging in the dirt. A child, his pants down around his ankles, crawled over the cracks in the sidewalk. Aside from us, he was the only human on the street; he crawled, fell, got up and crawled some more, his belly hard and distended. He didnt make a sound. When we passed him, he stopped and stared at us, his eyes wide in amazement. Dogs scattered in front of us and disappeared. But soon we came to the city proper. We met buses, bullock carts, other trishaws, trucks, and occasionally taxis. People appeared, walking and huddling in the shadows, swaying back and forth, sometimes singing. Their black mouths opened and closed as they swayed. The melodies rose and fell and joined with the music from wirelesses. The cripple had allowed his head to fall, it nodded with the motion of the trishaw. And soon, in spite of the slowness of the old man straining and sagging over the pedals, we arrived at the park. In the faint night light, it looked almost green; great pools of shadows lay on the ground; the trees bristled in the air, muttering at each passing breeze. Here and there dogs loped, silently, and young men in twos and threes walked endlessly in circles, chatting and giggling. They picked their way past piles of people who were sleeping. I nudged the cripple.

We're here, I said.

He looked up, frowning and blinking his eyes. He stared about. His head darted from side to side. His cheeks paled.

The p-p-park! he said.

Then his hand descended on my arm, clenching it.

Dont leave me! he said. A moment! Please! I was sleeping!

He took in great gulps of air, making hoarse noises in his throat. Then he leaned back, shut his eyes and relaxed his grip on me. He breathed more slowly. Drops of sweat trickled down his forehead. Around us several groups of young men had stopped. Their heads were all turned in our direction. But in a few minutes all the heads swiveled and stared at something else. Coming from my right, lumbering over the dry grass, was a large black-clothed man, his face white, his hands clasped behind his back. He nodded at the people he passed, and even at the sleeping figures on the ground. When he saw us, he stopped, and then strode directly towards me. He extended a hand and smiled widely. Hello, hello! he cried as he approached. How good to see you! Let me see, the atheist, am I right?

The cripple's eyes snapped open, but he remained leaning on the cushions.

Agnostic, I said.

Ah, of course, how foolish to forget! His yellowish eyes fastened on mine. Taking in the night air, eh? How lovely the park is, dont you agree?

Quite, I said. Youre taking the air yourself?

Yes, yes, meditating, you know! Eh? Ha-ha! Yes, we priests do meditate, it's the one thing we do rather well!

He slapped me on the knee with a big hand. The carriage rocked.

I come here quite often, you know, I enjoy the coolness of the evening, and talking to the young people. So refreshing! But where have you been these last several days, eh? I was looking forward to seeing you again, but you never came back to our little fete!

I've been busy, I said. And the girl?

Yes, she returned once more, with some friends. Such a lovely girl! We missed you terribly, you know. Yes, we did! She asked about you too. She seemed rather put out, if I may say so, eh?

He looked back and forth at us, his eyes becoming uncertain. The cripple was scowling at him. In the shadows all around us stood the young men, dark and silent and glittering. The priest cleared his throat. His gaze wandered off around the park, and his smile returned automatically to his mouth. All the time the trishaw driver hung motionless over his pedals. The priest turned to look at me again.

Refreshing, dont you think? he said. These young men. I've talked to several of them, you know. Such stimulating conversations! It's always a pleasure to meet such charming young people. Have you noticed the way they walk about in pairs, even holding hands? Such naiveté! In our countries, of course—but here! So—ingenuous, dont you think?

The cripple lurched forward; his eyes were red and burning; he spat out a stream of harsh, unrecognizable words, and the trishaw driver jerked upright, leaned heavily on his pedals, and, glancing over his shoulder, started moving us away. The priest raised a hand. He took a step forward. What's this? he said. I say.... But the trishaw picked up speed, moving through the park. The cripple leaned back and clenched his fists. His face was bright in the faint moonlight. I could hear him muttering, but couldnt make out the words. Then he leaned forward and shouted at the driver to stop. For a moment he stared at me. Then he spat over the side. Idiot! he said. The spittle lay white and weblike on the grass. He grabbed at his crutches. Idiot! he said again. Trembling, he pushed himself out of the carriage.

He turned to look at me once more, and then quickly levered himself away. Some young men moved off from the side to intercept him. Others drifted towards me. Their feet made no noise. The trishaw driver watched me. The young men slid over the grass, across the shadows, while the trees made whispering noises over their heads. I gestured at the trishaw driver, and we moved on, slowly. For a while young men followed us, smiles on their dark faces. Then we left the park. A street met us, gray and rough. A hotel moved past us, its courtyard deserted, the rooms lightless. Perhaps, I thought, no one lives there any more. I smiled at the old man pedaling me down the street. Finally I told him to stop. I got out and gave him some money. It's late, I told him. Shouldnt you go home? You look tired. He nodded his head. His eyes were half blind, his clothes torn and stained. Yes, Sahib, he said. But when I looked back, after walking a short distance, he was still there, collapsed over his handlebars.

IV.

The night was splashed with light: streetlamps, candles, naked bulbs in naked rooms, the stars burning overhead. I picked my way carefully over the sidewalks. I turned right, and left, and then perhaps right again. All the buildings looked the same. The stars did not move. But after a moment I heard footsteps behind me: the soft, gentle scrape of bare but tough feet being dragged over the concrete. I lowered my head, and put my hands in my pockets. I shuffled louder, and even whistled; I peered into the alleys and through the windows. But the steps followed me. When I turned, finally, I saw her, an old woman with a shawl over her head. One thin hand gathered the cloth under her chin; the other was held out in front, the palm up. Her dark lips were moving, but I could not hear any words, her lips moved, her eyes shone, her hand was held out, yet I could hear nothing but her bare feet scraping on the concrete. As she came closer her head nodded, and she smiled. I could see her thin arm trembling. I put a coin for her on the pavement and walked on. When she reached it, she leaned forward, squatted, and picked it up. Her mouth murmured. With great difficulty she got to her feet and continued following me. Her sari was dirty, cheap cloth. I put another coin on the ground. When she reached it, she squatted again, but when she tried to get up, she fell onto her side. She fell without sound, as lightly as a moth, onto her side. The hand holding the coin made little movements in front of her. The mouth opened and closed, the eyes bright. I watched her, and listened to the night, the burning of the stars, the clouds which swooped through the air. The woman's eyes were pleading with me. Her hands fluttered in front of her. A little wind flicked at the edges of her sari. I walked towards her, my sandals making clicking noises. When I reached her, I put one hand under her warm and dry armpit and without effort, a gentle tug, as though picking up a piece of paper, I lifted her to her feet.

Her lips murmured, and I could hear mewing sounds from her throat.

One horny hand patted my hair and my cheek, scratching my skin.

Teardrops formed in her eyes, glistening.

She murmured and mewed and patted my cheek and cried, gently, with the odors of curry and sweat steaming from her body. I took some coins and pressed them into her hand. She mewed and cried and patted me. When I left, she bowed to me, still making faint sounds in her throat, tears rolling down the deep scores in her cheeks.

Further on, a legless man strapped onto a wooden platform with wheels tried to sell me lottery tickets. He waved them in the air and shouted hoarsely. I walked on, but at the next corner I had to stop, there was a black gulf all around me. I trembled on the edge of the world. The legless man shot past me, propelling himself with fists against the ground, the wheels shooting sparks. In a moment he came roaring back, his eyes burning, lighting his way. The wind of his passing, the rush of his wheels, nearly knocked me over. I touched my fingers to a cold wall, and continued on my way.

I turned left, and right, and left again.

A naked child tottered down the street, his thumb in his mouth. Tears made little channels down his dirt-coated cheeks. His belly was hard and distended and there were scars and sores on his arms. He stared at me as I passed, his mouth shaped into a grimace as he sucked his thumb.

I turned right, then left, then perhaps right again.

A yellow pup came out of an alley next to me. There were fleas in his fur and ticks on his legs. I tried to help him, but he stumbled back into the alley and stood there, his belly heaving.

I turned left, then right, then left once more.

The legless man shot past me again, sparks flying from his eyes. The old woman held her shawl tightly over her head and mewed and cried. The child fell beside the dog. Men and women and shadows appeared, moving up and down the street. Trishaws tinkled, and a bald man cracked a whip, the cages spread in front of me, the buildings groaned and swayed, faces peered from behind slats and doorways. A taxi stopped, disgorging a few young Europeans. Ah-ha, I said to myself, we must be near the ocean, these men are sailors, I can tell. But the ocean was green and black and blue, the spray white, lifting from the tops of the swells. The ocean rolled and thundered against the beaches, against the ships, the cliffs that lined the sea. Down the street, in the darkness, rolled the trishaws; an occasional truck or bus thundered past; the wooden buildings swayed and cracked. In the little rooms at street level were the women, all of them. I peered through their windows and their open doors. They peered back at me; some smiled with their broken mouths, others cursed, some lifted their saris. A woman scratching herself was like a monkey:

her arms were long and hair grew from her knuckles. She swung from the bars and chattered. Next door was a woman bending over, her bare ass in the air. Baboon! I cried, and she bared her teeth at me also. A tiger paced up and down. A panther curled herself into a corner, licking her arms. It's time, I said, it's time you were fed and bedded down. And soon the keeper came. He was a small man with a red face and a bushy moustache, wearing a blue uniform complete with cap and gold braid. He pulled a cart loaded with meat and bananas and tasty scraps of food. He smiled at me and doffed his cap. Youre late, I told him, frowning. Right you are, he replied, it's late all right, that's for sure. He grinned and chewed on his moustache. He spat on the ground. Well? I said. What are you waiting for? Right you are, he said again, no use holding back, is it, mate? He winked at me and dug into his cart for a chunk of meat. All rightee! he cried. It's yer favorite time now, mateys! No pushin or youll get a chunk down yer throat!

A chorus of snarls and growls rose into the air. He threw a chunk of meat into the nearest cage, and the panther leaped onto it, her teeth glittering. She pulled it to one side and stared at us suspiciously as she ate, her throat making huge gulping movements. Into the cage with the monkey the keeper threw bananas, lettuce leaves, and coffee grounds. The monkey made che-che-che noises, swinging from a bar with her tail, and thumbed her nose at us. Her eyes were small and red. Hey-hey now, said the keeper. None of that or you wont get none at all next time! The monkey made an obscene gesture, and a bear spat at us. Goddamn bastids, the keeper muttered, chewing on his moustache. He shook a fist in the air. Go on now! he shouted. Yer nothin but a bunch of bloody mongrels! He turned to me. Cant talk no sense to em, he muttered. I knock my ass off carrying this stuff, and look what thanks I get! He threw some more meat, and the animals snarled and clamored. They shook the bars of their cages, their eyes wild and ferocious. The keeper picked up a stick and went from cage to cage, slapping at their paws. Get on with you! he shouted. Knock off that noise! He threw into the cages meat, beer bottles, slats of wood, liver, chicken feathers, assorted bones, and crumpled-up balls of paper. The animals tore and ripped, growling and barking and chattering, spitting at the little man. His face got redder and redder. He chewed angrily at his moustache, and hit at the bars with his stick. The hair at the back of his neck was standing up straight. Finally he came back to me and kicked the side of his cart. Look at em! he said. You ever see nothing like it? I shrugged. Theyre sick and hungry, I said. He snorted. Mongrels, that's what they are, he said, bloody useless mongrels! He dug into his cart and came up with a beer bottle. Have some, he said, but I shook my head. He gulped the liquid down and wiped his lips. Cant keep themselves clean, he went on, cant work—look at em!—got no pride, no sense at all. Mongrels! He yanked at his moustache, reached into the cart for a sandwich, and chewed noisily. He finished his beer and threw the bottle into a cage.

They dont know any better, I said.

Dont know any better! he mimicked. What are you, some kind of nut?

All their lives, I said.

All their lives! he scoffed. What we oughta do is feed em arsenic! Drop a bomb on em! Theyre no use to us. All they do is cause trouble. The world would be better off without em!

Youd be better off, you mean, I said.

Sure, he said. Why not? We're civilized, anyway.

I stared at him. He pulled out another beer bottle and drained it. He threw it into a cage, where it broke, spattering glass everywhere.

Gotta be goin, he said. Got a little honey waitin for me. She's black, but what the hell, theyre all good for a lay, eh?

He laughed and slapped me on the shoulder. He disappeared. The cart vanished.

I went up the stairs of the whorehouse. I climbed slowly, dragging my feet. I tried to count the steps, but it was impossible, the numbers confused me. In the end, numberless, I struggled to the top anyway. There were few women in the room: the two hairy peasant girls holding hands, the one with the cleft lip, and the mama, who was sleeping, sagging back in her chair. I nudged her and she awoke, her eyes flicking open. She did not move, but only stared at me.

It is late, she said.

I know.

It is almost morning.

Yes, youre right.

The girls are asleep.

I will awaken her.

Thirty rupees, she said.

All the time her eyes stayed on mine. Her lips only barely moved. The two peasant girls nodded sleepily and the harelip stared straight in front of her. The broad bottom of the mama overflowed the seat of her chair. When I gave her the money, she stuffed it into her bosom, between the huge fat breasts, and immediately shut her eyes. A snore came from between her motionless lips. I tip-toed across the room, passing the mirror: for a moment I was caught in it, halted in mid-stride, a red face, dry pale hair, a wiry beard. My eyes looked fearfully at the eyes staring back at me. Then I slid past. My foot descended, and the mirror showed only the wall of the room and the sleeping fat woman. I crept softly down the corridor until I came to her door; the darkness was as soft as feathers, grazing my cheeks. I opened her door. She was asleep on the bed, her legs curled, one arm flung out. She was naked and her hair had fallen around her face. She looked warm and soft, her eyelids and thighs and breasts moist. When I shut the door she awoke. She squinted her eyes up at me, and opened her mouth in a scowl. As she spoke, her voice full of sleep, foggy and muffled, she moved her arms so she was leaning back on her elbows; the slight motion made her breasts tremble, and little drops of sweat coursed into the hollow between them; her thighs followed after her torso, rolling over, and her legs parted momentarily to show her stiffly curled pubic hair and the plump lips of her vagina; and as she rolled, her eyes squinting, her forehead frowning, she spoke, muffled and angry:

Is too late—why you come here?

PART FOUR

I.

My room is a dungeon; I have banished myself. But
the decision was taken so long ago, it is difficult to remember the reasons. Outside, through my single window, I see
only haze, and at times, late in the afternoon, the red dust
that comes sweeping through the sky. There are never any
birds, they do not come here; the land is dead. Only the
persistent flies, the insects, flock around this city, in numbers that seem to grow each day. I stare through the yellow
glass, and wander about the room with my eyes. On the
walls I find a map of the world: the continents, the oceans,
the inland seas, black rivers, icy mountains, the sandy hills
around Aliminos Bay, the jungle around Lahad Datu, the
flat, diseased land at Exmouth Gulf, the peaks of Nuku
Hiva; they are written in the urine stains, the broken plaster, the long cracks that wind through valleys and gorges,
along the discolored countries. What is there to say? I have
been everywhere. I find the red-painted Masai plains. The
endless mornings line up behind each other. Light comes
through a single window: gray and yellow and red, cold
and warm and hot. Outside I hear noises, bullock carts,
buses, people talking, the slap of their feet. Ah, I say, I am
here, I am safe. I feel my mind turning and twisting. Images and visions poke forward, they thrust themselves in

front of me. The cripple says: You are well fed, pampered, and rich. But I feel my arms and legs and chest. I am wasting away. The son says: Why do you drink arak? Why not whiskey, in your own country? Why do you come here? He stands in the park, the wind whipping his long white shirt. It is easy to smile and move off. My eyes can slip past him, and look at the trees. So much blood! cries a woman, but there was no blood, only sand and pain. The whore looks at me. Her small body twists in her bed, one arm thrown out, her eyes hooded with sleep. Is too late, she says, why you come here? But I tell her to move over. I lie beside her and dream of the ocean that came leaping against the cliffs. I hunted for crabs beneath the flat rocks, in the little pools of water. The girl sat, trembling with the roar of the sea.

I'm leaving you, she said. Youve destroyed me, but you wont get any satisfaction out of it.

The crabs eluded me, the flat rocks were empty.

Why do you need to wander? she asked. Youre never satisfied with anything. Why dont you stop, for a while? How long do you think I can go on like this? You never think of me.

Is that true? I asked. Have I destroyed you?

Her eyes became flat and gray.

I'm leaving you, she said. When I get to Durbin, I'm going home.

I struggled with a huge rock, trying to tip it over. But it was too heavy. Defeated, I lay in the sun and let the heat work its way into me. After a while we returned to the road and sat by our packs. All around us the country was flat and dry, the earth red, a few scrubs struggling through the soil. We waited in the dust until a truck stopped. We threw our packs on back and climbed up. Watching us were two dark Masai with spears, wearing sheets of orange cloth. Their hair was crusted with mud. The driver and his companion wore shirts and short pants, and they grinned at us, full of teeth. Also on back were two fifty gallon drums of oil and one small black lamb. As the truck bounced down the track, the lamb stumbled and sprawled about, making tiny bleating noises. All the time the girl sat, curled up, grimacing at each bump. The dust from the truck's passage stirred and whipped around us, coating our hair, our eyes, our skin damp from the heat. It was late in the afternoon before we stopped and were let out; they were going bush, down a narrow track, away from the road. The driver grinned and waved at us. The Masai lifted their spears. The lamb bleated and stumbled. The two drums of oil made loud booming noises.

Alongside the road were three mud huts.

We stood there, the small silent girl and myself.

After a while a car approached, going south, with a white woman driving. It did not stop. Later, as evening came, a truck passed us going north, and the people in it waved. I returned their greeting, but the girl only squatted, motionless, staring at her feet. Then she crossed the road and went into the bush. When she came back her face was pinched and shiny with sweat. She found some shade under a small tree, and rested there with her eyes shut.

As it grew darker three Africans came and stood around one of the huts. When I went up to them, they smiled. Two were old, with grizzled faces, and the other was only a child. The oldest man was crippled, and the other spoke English. He had a thin white beard, little curls of coarse hair lying flat against his cheeks and chin. I asked him if we could sleep in one of the huts. He showed me one which was empty, and volunteered to give us his bed. I refused. We had sleeping bags, we were used to the ground, we had no wish to make him uncomfortable. He went into his hut and came out with two bottles of soft drinks which he opened with his teeth. I took one to the girl, but she shook her head. My stomach is bothering me, she said. The drinks were warm, but I drank both of them, slowly. By the time I finished, it was dark. I took our packs into the hut and spread out our sleeping bags. The roof was thatch, dry and rustling and full of spider webs, and the ground was slightly damp, but it was a place to sleep, away from the stars which burned in the black sky, away, I thought, away from the dark flat plains, the walls cut them off. Inside was an area closely defined. I could pace from wall to wall. It was simple, sharp and clear. But the girl sniffed at the moisture and the musky air and glowered at me. She flung herself onto her sleeping bag, her back to me, her legs sprawled. Her hair fell over her face. It's only for one night, I whispered. Tomorrow we'll reach the border, maybe even Lusaka; it'll be easier then.

Leave me alone, she said.

Do you remember? I said. Do you remember Fiji? The little apartment we had in Suva?

She was silent.

Do you remember the hills, how beautiful they were, with the flowers growing everywhere?

She said nothing. The hut was dark and damp. I could feel the walls rather than see them. The roof made rustling noises: insects, perhaps, or perhaps just the wind moving in the thatch.

That was a long time ago, she said after a moment.

Yes, a long time ago.

Later it began to rain. It came softly at first, only a light patter on the straw roof, but I was still awake and heard it. Then the wind suddenly rose; it drove in across the flat plains, from the west, and brought with it a sudden flood. The noise awakened the girl, and she stared at the leaking roof and then at me, with bitter eyes. She sat upright. The earth turned into a swamp. The trees dragged their beards on the ground. Then the rain stopped, except for a drizzle, and there was only the wind.

II.

I have not seen the whore for a long time: I no longer go out. There is no need to try to escape these walls and the map inscribed on them, since everywhere I go they exist. And perhaps she has, by now, moved to another house, or died; they move about a lot, from house to house, they fight with the mamas or get tired of the same scenery, and they are always dying. The trishaw driver, I'm sure, is dead also. He no longer comes by, ringing his bell and calling out to me; no more do I hear Sahib, Sahib cried in a thin voice. His trishaw will be sold, or stolen, or given to one of his sons so the boy may earn a living when he comes of age—although the child may never come of age. The old man who lives in this house has either died or disappeared. The son will not tell me, he only shrugs his shoulders, and his mother looks at me with distrust. Why do you come here? she asked. You have stayed many weeks; why do you not go? She is gray and her body is weightless; all her strength is in her voice. I smile at her when she comes to my door. I have become a curse; she no longer brags about the white Sahib who stays in her house. Some day she will kick me out, she will evict me, I will be thrown into the street like a landless peasant. It amuses me to think about it. I imagine her standing there, shaking with rage—and fear, too, for I am a white Sahib— and ranting at me. No, I answer, I am not lazy. No, I am not broke, not yet. I have more money than you will see in a year, I have carefully folded it and hidden it in a secret pocket. And I have worked all over the world, hard, laborious jobs, work none of you could manage. I grew up with hard work. I grew up in a house on a flat land, which is how our name was derived, and I worked on my father's land from sunrise to sunset, or perhaps later. I worked all summer, and in the winter trudged to school, and worked in the evenings and holidays. When I became older I stopped. I would not work. Our land, from whence

we derived our name, meant nothing to me. It was not
enough to have a name. I would be free.

Why you come here? the gray woman asked.

I traveled all around the world, and attached to my
name a list of countries and oceans, villages and seas. When
the name became too long, when it became cumbersome, I
attached to it another person. She was small and gentle.
She was sweet, and had shining eyes. She was eager to see
the list of countries, the rest of my name, and I took her on
a voyage which ended, two years later, in Africa. During
that time: her eyes lost their luster; her body shrank; her
limbs became limp; her voice turned into a whine or a snarl
and finally a cry; her vagina dried, she became barren, she
bled once a month, cold or hot, hungry or well fed; her hair
became twisted, she cut it short, and no longer did I comb
it, holding her naked on my knee; her breasts turned thin
and flat, though before they had swung over my face, the
nipples squeezed and sucked, the legs caressed, the belly
rubbed while her mouth made pleasurable noises; she no
longer ran, she walked, the heat no longer passed over her
but bit deeply into her flesh, new mountains and new
oceans could no longer raise a sparkle in her eye or a shine
to her face. She defecated, usually once a day, and with
increasing pain and secretiveness. In Olongapo she went
with an American sailor, but she ran back to me and cried.
In Kota Belud we lay on a bed in a rest house and smiled at
the mountain called Kinabalu. A stream ran in the valley
before us. The mountain peak was black with rock. In
Penang we huddled in the shadows, waiting for the ship to
take us to Madras. I could smell food cooking but I gave
her rice. In Dhanashkodi we looked at the wooden shacks.
Her frightened face was turned towards the sea. After we
left, a typhoon demolished the town. In Nurye Elia the mist
formed on her body, and she shivered with the cold. But
she bled in spite of it, it was that time of the month. She
bled while we looked at the monkey temple. She bled while
we were crowded into a bus full of Sengalese. In Mombasa

she hated the noise and the dirt and the rough hotel in which we stayed. Come south, I said, come south, it's better there. I herded her down the road. I did not want to lose part of my name. Near the ocean I hunted for crabs in the little pools of water.

I'm leaving you, she said. When I get to Durbin I'm going home. Youve destroyed me, but you wont get any satisfaction out of it. Look at me. Youve made me dry and bitter. No one will want me now.

Stay with me, I said. I know, I know. But I cant go on like this forever, either. Someday we'll have peace.

Peace, she said.

Then she whispered: Do you hate me so much?

I struggled with a rock, trying to turn it over, but it was too heavy. Then we got a ride in a truck. At three mud huts were three black people, two old and one young. The boy had sores on his arms. He was shy and hid from us, but later I caught him smiling at me. The old man who spoke English was his father, he had a sort of store, with canned goods and soft drinks and potatoes and rice, and the natives from the villages in the bush around us would sometimes come in and buy from him. He had a small yellow pup with ticks on his legs and lice in his fur, and as I talked I tried to pet the dog, but he tottered away from me and stood in a bit of shade, his belly heaving. The dog is frightened of strangers, said the old man. He led me to a hut which was empty. The other old man was half blind and walked with the aid of a stick. The one who spoke English was still husky, but the other had become thin and stooped, his hair had turned white, and his face was only bone and skin, like a dried skull. The hut was moist, and the roof looked like it would leak. My oldest son lived here with his wife, said the African. What happened to them? I asked. He shrugged. They all go to the city, he said. They will not stay in the bush any more. All the young people go to the city to starve and drink pombe. Progress, I said. I am an old man, he answered. It is nothing. Your people have

changed our ways, but soon I will die. There will be many
changes yet, after I am gone. Bwana, he added. When it
became darker I took our packs into the hut and spread
our sleeping bags. The oldest man came to the door of the
hut and tried to peer in, to see what I was doing. He spoke
to me, but it was not English or Swahili, so I did not understand him. After a while he went away, leaning on his stick.
During the night it rained. The girl looked at me with bitter eyes. When the hardest rain stopped, it still drizzled for
a long time, and then that stopped too, and there was only
the wind rushing through the few trees and fingering the
thatch of our roof. In the morning the wind stopped momentarily. The ground was a rich, red mud. The air was
very clear, and I could see for miles in all directions. The
girl remained in the hut, saying she didnt feel well, so I
took our packs out and let them dry in the sun. By mid-day
the mud had dried. The sky was pale blue, almost white,
and the day had become humid, full of moisture from the
ground. I bought some tinned meat from the African and
took it into the hut.

Are you hungry? I asked the girl.

In the darkness her face looked very young. She was
sweating slightly. She shook her head.

Youd better eat something, I said.

I dont want anything.

How about some tea?

She didnt say anything so I went out and gathered
wood. I boiled the water in a big tin and got some canned
milk from the old man. I mixed her tea with a little milk
and a little sugar. When I returned to the hut, her eyes were
shut. She was lying on top of the sleeping bag, wearing a
pair of tight, soiled white pants and a white brassiere. Her
skin was dark, well tanned, her hair black and slightly
tangled.

How do you feel? I asked.

She took the tea and sipped at it.

Is it serious, you think? I asked.

It's only my stomach, she said. She looked at me, her eyes soft. Will we get to Lusaka today?

I dont know, I said. I doubt therell be much traffic, because of the rain.

I went back outside. Lusaka was still a long ways; even on a good day we would never have made it, although we might have reached the border. I waited, but there was no traffic, and late in the afternoon the wind started again, this time bringing dust instead of rain.

III.

At the hut in Africa the dust blew all night; here, it blows only for a few hours. It comes sometimes in the afternoon, like a great yellow beast, leaping onto the city, snarling and spitting and choking the people. During these hot afternoons the sky is dirty and coarse and sullen, and the dust in the air makes the sunsets heavy and red. The color swirls and rushes about, the sun bleeds through the sky, and when night finally falls, and the wind dies, the stars can only barely be seen. During these times the people in the streets are hushed and uneasy. I myself, when I still walked about, walked uncertainly. The buildings were ready to fall. They leaned over me, grimacing with their ancient pains. It was easy to get lost, at first, since the streets had no names: no signs on the corners, no arrows, the doorways without numbers. The air was filled with the snapping and cracking of wood. Old women crossed their arms over their dry breasts. The wind tugged at their saris, the wind made them sway and falter as they ran across the streets. In Africa, there was only the girl in the hut, the old man with the stick (walking crookedly, grinning toothlessly), the old man who spoke English (whose son and son's wife had gone to the city to starve and drink pombe), the young boy, a mere child with sores on his arm, and myself. There was also a little yellow dog. When the wind started in the afternoon, bringing the clouds of dust, the dog disappeared, perhaps into one of the huts. The oldest man remained hidden. The old man who spoke English came to see me; I sat at the entrance to our hut, where I could watch both the girl and the road. All day there had been no traffic, but the heat had dried the mud, and it was possible that some cars had started south before the dust storm. Behind the old man was the boy. He crouched under the wind. The old man's face was covered with yellow dust. He squatted beside me.

You have picked a bad time to come here, he said.
I nodded.
How long do these storms last? I asked
Sometimes many days. How is your woman?
She doesnt feel well.

His eyes were old and quiet. He rocked a little on his heels, blinking his eyes at the dust. The boy leaned against his back, putting his arms around the man's neck. I could see the puckered eruptions; the juices from the sores were caked with dirt. The wind made the trees whistle.

But when evening came, everything turned red and the wind died. The air became heavy. The land, flat and ochre, spread to the darkening horizon. The girl remained on her sleeping bag; the dust had covered her sweating body, and I took a damp rag and washed her. I've been sick before, she said. It always passes. Where does it hurt? I asked. She pressed her abdomen with a small hand.

Outside, the old man had gathered wood for a fire. I watched him, the girl, and the road. The yellow pup came up to the fire, and the boy caught it; he searched through the ragged fur for lice. Each time he found one, he held it up with a smile on his face and then threw it into the fire. The burning wood cracked and snapped, and I thought I could also hear the lice as they burst from the heat. The oldest man walked up, leaning on his stick. His voice was thin and querulous, the voice wavered, just like his walk, from side to side. The old man who spoke English helped him sit. Then he brought out a pipe and smoked silently, while the boy lifted the lice proudly and threw them into the fire. After a while I asked if the wind would start up again, and the old man nodded. I brought some food to the girl, but she still refused to eat. Then I went to the fire and made some more tea. The pup tried to wiggle away at my approach, but the boy held him tight and smiled at me. It's very beautiful here, I said, and the old man nodded again. The oldest man smiled vacantly. His mouth was empty. I could hear the fire and the lice sputtering, and far in the distance, perhaps, a few animals, but the sounds were too faint, and I could not concentrate on them. I tried to dream, but the countries I had traveled through had disappeared, they had vanished from my mind. There was only a mixture of smells and colors. I am confused, I said to myself. The old man nodded his head sleepily, puffing at his pipe. I took deep breaths, but the lingering dust hurt my lungs. The flames of the fire flickered with the beginnings of a breeze. The old man sighed and looked at me. I listened, and far off the ground began to stir; the trees, far away, quivered; high over my head I could see the stars blink out, bunches at a time. I went back into the hut. The girl gripped my hand. Her eyes were closed. I could hear the wind again, and dust blew through the doorway.

IV.

Around me was a dry red land. The air was yellow, and red. Inside the hut was darkness: I strung a sheet across the doorway and filled the cracks with paper and clothes. Still, the dust ate its way inside, it filtered through the thatch roof and under the eaves and around the flapping sheet. I lit a candle so we could see, but often it went out as the trailing wind caught it. Always it flickered. Shadows leapt over the walls. On her sleeping bag, the girl brightened and darkened. Her hair was full of grit. Her body I wiped with a damp cloth, I took off her clothes and sponged her down, but it did little good. Perhaps the coolness made her feel better. She spoke sometimes while I washed her. Where are we? she asked. Will we get to Lusaka today? Once she said, I'm leaving you. And she added: Please. Her voice became smaller than her body. Her little feet hung awkwardly at the ends of her legs. I wiped between her toes and around her heels. Her legs remained firm and strong, although her voice wasted away, and sweat constantly broke out on her face. On the second night in the hut she passed water; her muscles, perhaps, gave way; the urine smell spread through the close air, but I did not think she noticed it. In the morning I carefully cleaned her. I washed the small patch of hair on her groin. I gave her my sleeping bag, picking her up and laying her down again, a slight, lax body. In the candlelight her belly looked swollen, shiny and hard. Her eyes flickered open and shut.

During the morning the old man came to see me. He peered through the dimness at the girl. Was there anything he could do? I asked if there was a doctor anywhere nearby, but he shook his head. In Dodoma, perhaps, he said. But that was a long way. It would do little good to try to walk there. But sometimes there was a truck in one of the villages, and he could send his son to find out. If so, the girl could be driven to Dodoma, or even Arusha. We can try, I told him. When he left I went out to the road. I dragged a log across it and piled up some bushes, so if anyone came he would have to stop. The wind blew all around me; a clump of trees across the road made loud, rushing noises, and the bushes I piled kept blowing away. I finally anchored them with rocks and another log. Everything was a yellowish red. I could only feel the sun, overhead, beating at me.

I went back into the hut.

We've sent for a truck, I told her. Perhaps we can get you to Dodoma tonight, where there's a doctor.

She looked up at me, her eyes wide open. Her forehead was very hot.

Where are we? she asked.

In a little village.

Will we get to Lusaka today?

I hope so.

She shut her eyes. I dampened a rag and put it on her forehead. After a while the old man came to the hut, followed by his son. The boy's eyes were big and bright. He stared in awe at the girl lying half naked on the ground. I am sorry, the old man said. I looked at him. He turned to the boy and patted him. The truck, he said, is not in the village. It had already left. The boy had sent some people after it, but it might be a long time before they found the truck. It did not follow a regular route, and it was very hard for the people to travel through the storm. They were dependable, they were strong and tireless walkers, but it would be difficult. The truck was old, too, he said, and often it would break down for days at a time. He let his eyes turn to the girl. Whenever he moved, the dust trickled from his face and arms, and fell silently onto the earth. Outside, above and around his voice, the wind was shouting. It came leaping from the west, across the plains, moving like a loud, swift animal, sniffing at the trees, scattering bushes, raking at the ground. It blew the dirt into the air. It carried away the roofs of houses, and sent the cattle and sheep mad. Every year, the old man said, the wind came, sometimes later and sometimes earlier. In a few weeks it would bring the monsoon rains. He became silent, rocking a little on his heels. The boy put his arms around the man's neck, and stared from me to the girl. She lay tense and sweating on the sleeping bag. Her mouth opened and closed, as though finding difficulty in breathing, and sometimes she made moaning noises. Her hands moved across her body, pulling and plucking. The old man got to his feet. I will bring you some more water, he said. He looked at me for a moment. I am an old man, he said. For me, death would be almost a pleasant thing. But for someone so young, it is not easy. He went out, but his words remained in the hut, and for a long time I could only listen to his voice and the voice of the wind.

When he returned, with a covered basin of water, he said some people had come. They are from the village, he said. They were very curious. Many of them had never seen a white woman. But he would keep them away from the hut. Perhaps they thought they could help, their presence, their noise, could scare away the sickness. They had walked for many miles through the storm. When I went to the door I saw them. I pulled back the sheet and stepped outside, and there they were, perhaps a dozen of them, tall dark figures blurred by the dust. Some wore orange robes, like the Masai wore, and others were in trousers and ragged shirts. When they saw me they nodded their heads and stomped their feet on the ground. These are not Masai, said the old man. They are only a small tribe, and they are dying out. I nodded back at them. The wind flapped at their clothes. I went back inside. The girl stared straight at me. Why have you turned out the light? she said. I brought the candle closer to her. Why did you go away? she said. Did you have to go so far? I dampened the rag with the water the old man had brought and washed her face. That feels good, she said. Youre very kind to me, arent you? Youve never shouted at me, or hit me. She shut her eyes and her mouth opened and closed. I'm a bitch, she said. No, I said. I am, she repeated. I always was. Why did you want me, when you knew I was a bitch? I moved to get the basin. Where are you going? she said. Youre going away again! No, I said, I'm only getting more water. Yes, she said, it's very hot. What's all that noise? Is there someone outside? I shook my head. It's the wind, I said. Her hands plucked at her belly. I took both of them in one of my hands and put the damp rag on her stomach. Is that better? I asked. Dont leave me, she said. Stay here. Dont go away again. I cant stand it when you go away.

I've never left you, I said.

You do. Youve always left me. You just stand there, and go away.

Then she pulled her hands free from mine and gripped her belly. She arched her back a little, turning to one side, her eyes shut. It hurts, she whispered. Then she fell back down. Her hair, over her forehead, was damp with sweat. Her cheeks looked red in the candlelight. As the afternoon passed, her body seemed to grow heavier, and the small lines around her eyes, placed there by laughter, became deeper and darker. Her cheeks were pockets of shadows. She kept pushing at her pants, so finally I took them off, leaving only her thin white briefs, and placed a damp towel over her. Towards evening the old man came in. As he pushed aside the sheet, the dust swirled past him, and I caught a glimpse of the small group of natives. He wiped the dust from his mouth. Some more people have come, he said. They know nothing of the truck. His heavy arms lay across his knees. A long shadow fell behind him, changing shape as the candle flickered. Can I bring you anything? he asked. I am cooking some food. You, at least, will have to eat. I shook my head. Not now, I said. Perhaps tonight the wind will stop, and some cars will come. In the morning, he said, I will send my son to the village again. Perhaps there will be news of the truck. I thanked him and he left. A few moments later he returned with a plate covered with newspaper. The plate held small pieces of meat and a few yams. I ate while I watched the girl and listened to the wind. Sometimes I could hear the natives singing. But the noise of the wind was always there. It faded, sometimes, and the sheet would not flap so badly, but it always returned. As the night progressed, it seemed to grow worse. It will blow itself out, I said. The old man shook his head. He hadnt moved. Perhaps, he said. It can blow for a week. What sickness do you think it is? I am not a doctor, I said. It could be almost anything. But you have had shots? he asked. I nodded. But it could be something else. Perhaps the shots did not take. Perhaps her appendix. Food poisoning. Once she had dysentery. That was in India, I remembered, and it had been more uncomfortable than anything else. A doctor had given her some medicine which cured it very quickly; or else her body had simply thrown it off.

You are English? asked the old man. Many young Englishmen come to this country.

I shook my head. In a lull of the wind I heard the natives singing.

There are few of them left, he said. So many of the young people go to the city. Even among the Masai.

Everything changes, I said.

Yes, he said. But it makes an old man bitter. I do not trust the white man. You will forgive me. But I do not trust him.

The wind blew, the candle burned down, and the old man got me a new one. Perhaps I slept. There was noise, only the changing light, the girl's body. The dust blew through the holes in the walls, under the eaves, sifting through the straw roof. From the corner of my eye I could see the sheet flapping, the bottom of it curling upward and then snapping down. Towards morning the girl's breathing became hard. She opened and closed her mouth, and made rough rasping noises in her throat. I took her hands and held them. The old man squatted there, dark and silent. The morning was very red and loud. When I went outside, the natives were grouped silently in the lee of the next hut. A few of them stirred as they saw me, but they said nothing.

While it was still early the old man sent his son out again. I watched him go, a small dark figure with an old rag wrapped around his head. He quickly disappeared, the dust closing around him. He was gone all morning. During this time the girl became steadily weaker. I could see it in the way she moved; her hands lifted very slowly, she breathed heavily, her face sagged and her jaw dropped open so I could see her small teeth and her tongue. When I tried to give her water she nearly choked. The water ran from the corners of her lips, across her cheeks and made dark spots on the sleeping bag. She no longer talked, she made mumbling noises, though once, when I put my ear close to her, I thought I heard her say, Help me. I could not be sure. Help me. And her hands came slowly off the sleeping bag, raised a few inches, and fell again. She turned her face from side to side. I could hear the breath in her throat. I could do nothing but wash her, hold her hand, and lift her head to give her water. Then, early in the afternoon, when the heat could be felt burning through the air, the old man came in with his son. The boy's chest was heaving and his arms trembling, as though he had been running. The old man shook his head. The truck has gone many miles away, he said. It was in a village very far from here, unless they had gone on already. Some people had gone to get it, but even if they reached it tonight, the truck could not return for another day. They could not drive fast over the trail, hardly faster than a good man could walk; the springs would break. But they would try. I thanked both of them, and they left. Outside the natives were chanting. The wind blew, the dust drove against their bodies, but they stamped their feet and sang. The dust fell, and I wiped it away. The candle flickered and the darkness wavered. The air was very dry and hot. When I sat too long, my legs cramped, and I had to walk up and down in the little space.

Late in the afternoon she lifted up, and her eyes opened wide, bright and staring straight in front of her. When she fell back down, her hands came alive, they threw off the towel and clawed at her belly. A long, dry sound came from her chest, through her throat, a series of low grunts. Her body jerked. She grunted and jerked while I watched her, and then calmly relaxed and lay still. Her eyes and mouth remained open. I felt for a pulse, and then listened for her breath. After a while I shut her eyes. I moved her head a little, so her body was straight, and closed her jaws. Then I sat there for a long time. The old man came in, and left without saying anything. Sometime during the night the candle went out. The walls of the hut were very dark. I could barely see her lying flat on the sleeping bag, and she looked weightless to me. The wind moved her hair, and her body drifted as the wind touched her. She rose to the ceiling, and went from wall to wall. She passed gently in front of me, her hair long again and trailing behind her. She was merely a white shadow with black hair. She wore thin white panties, and a white brassiere. Then she turned red. The whole hut turned faintly red. The color crept in from under the eaves, it drifted past the white sheet. It settled onto my head and arms and washed over the girl. There was no noise—the redness was silent, the air did not stir—and after a moment I realized the wind had stopped. Later that morning it rained a little, only a light spattering, enough to clear the air and make the ground shine and glitter. I went outside. The natives gathered a short distance from me. Far in the distance I could see hills, purple ridges rising above the plains. It was the first time I had seen them. The three huts were small and quiet. I borrowed a shovel from the old man.

You had better wait, he said. The authorities will want to see her.

It has nothing to do with the authorities, I said.

But in the end I couldnt do it. I left the shovel lying on the ground and went back to the hut. The truck arrived in the afternoon, and the old man went to Dodoma and brought back a group of white people and some Africans dressed in business suits. They stood around and talked. They took her passport. A doctor argued with another man, and they poked and pried and asked me questions. Several people made speeches without seeming to realize it. They stood tall and strong, and made gestures with their hands. I sat off by myself. A clean sheet was brought from somewhere, and they wrapped it around the girl. The men in business suits stood around me. Behind them were the natives from the bush, dressed in all different colors, some red, some green or yellow or black. Dark shoes scraped at the ground. One man became angry, and another led him away. Others shook my hand, as though congratulating me. They patted me on the back. I stared at them. Long white teeth were shining in the sunlight. Hair lay flat and dead on white heads, and tight and curled on dark heads. Goodbye, I told them. One man began arguing again, so I gave him some money. They all came around and shook my hand once more and patted me on the back. They nodded and coughed. Then they all got in their cars, putting the girl, wrapped in her sheet, across the seat of one of them, and drove off. The dust raised behind them, and died. The oldest man, with his white hair, leaning on his stick, came from his hut and stared at me, as though trying to memorize my face. The old man who spoke English took him away. The natives all left.

Towards evening a car came, going north, and gave me a ride. It was driven by two white South Africans wearing bush jackets and soft, crooked hats. The small huts, the red earth and the purple ridge of mountains were left behind, but a few days later they appeared again in front of me. I changed direction. I worked my way through crowds of dark people. I crossed the ocean in a small sailboat, driven east by the monsoon winds, and landed in a country full of yellow dust. Later I got a ride on the back of a lorry, stuffed in among sacks of manure and chicken feathers and piles of refuse. The days on the road dried and withered me. I looked at my long red hands. Then we arrived in a city. The streets were dark and disorganized and without name, they ran off in all directions, filled with people and rubble. I found a place to stay. There is no point in going on, I told myself. I stretched my arms and legs. The evening spread all around me. The twilight turned everything purple. I nodded at my reflection in the window. Let there be peace, I told it. My face nodded back at me. Let there be peace.